Mrs Morell

The Catholic Church

an epitome of sacred history

Mrs Morell

The Catholic Church
an epitome of sacred history

ISBN/EAN: 9783741194160

Manufactured in Europe, USA, Canada, Australia, Japa

Cover: Foto ©Andreas Hilbeck / pixelio.de

Manufactured and distributed by brebook publishing software
(www.brebook.com)

Mrs Morell

The Catholic Church

THE

CATHOLIC CHURCH:

AN EPITOME

OF

SACRED HISTORY.

EDINBURGH
PRINTED BY BALLANTYNE AND COMPANY,
PAUL'S WORK.

THE

CATHOLIC CHURCH:

AN EPITOME

OF

SACRED HISTORY.

BY MRS MORELL.

Third Edition.

EDINBURGH:

WILLIAM P. NIMMO, 2 ST DAVID STREET.

LONDON: SIMPKIN, MARSHALL, & CO.

M.DCCC.LX.

DEAR MRS MORELL,

I have perused your little book with great pleasure, and I shall warmly recommend its adoption within the Catholic Schools of this vicariate. As a short, lucid, and judiciously-classed Text-book of Church History, it very opportunely supplies one of the many deficiencies yet felt in our school library; while the foot-notes with which you have enriched its every page, stamp it at once an elementary work in perfect harmony with the most approved system of teaching of the present day. The few slightly inaccurate expressions of the original French can easily be rectified in the next edition, which I feel satisfied will soon be called for; and which, I trust, may and will prove but the forerunner of many others.

Allow me, moreover, to say, that to me not the least interesting feature in your little volume, is the good example it conveys to many of our Catholic ladies of talent and education as to the useful employment of their leisure hours. To the credit of the Catholic ladies of England, this is not the first good example of the kind that has been given of late years; let us hope that it will not be the last.

I need scarcely add that, should you think fit to do so, you are at perfect liberty to make any public use you please of this letter.

Believe me,

Yours truly in Christ,

✠ JAS. GILLIS,
*Bp. Vic. Ap. of the Eastern District
in Scotland.*

To Mrs MORELL,
Greenhill Gardens, Edinburgh.

THE CATHOLIC CHURCH:

AN EPITOME OF SACRED HISTORY.

THE Church of Rome has only to relate her history, in order to instruct man according to the will of God, and to lead him to a knowledge of the truth. The dogmas to be received, the precepts to be observed, the worship to be practised, have all been successively revealed and developed; these communications being always proportioned to the requirements of each succeeding generation.

There is no instruction more important or more reliable than a knowledge of events. It is impossible to be deceived when proofs rest upon facts. Moreover, the history of leading events, from the beginning up to the present time, is the history of the *Catholic* [1] *Church*, and it is thus named because it extends from all times and to all places.

The substance of this little work is taken from a French book, entitled, " L'Echelle Catholique," by M. L'Abbé J. B. A. A., and the Bishop of Oregon, which was first brought under our notice, and highly recommended as a useful epitome, by the Sisters of Notre Dame.

As a short, plain work of this description is much wanted at the present day, and nothing of the kind appears to exist in English, it has occurred to us that it might be useful to the faithful and others, to present it in an English dress, with such alterations and additions as were demanded in order to make it better adapted for circulation in Great Britain and Ireland.

Etymological foot-notes have been added for the use of teachers, and as an aid to those who wish to improve themselves in the knowledge of the derivation of English words.

CONTENTS.

ANCIENT HISTORY.

MEDIEVAL HISTORY.

MODERN HISTORY.

NAMES OF AUTHORS CONSULTED IN THE PRESENT WORK.

BICKMORE (Rev. C.), Chronological Tables. Third Edition. 1857.

BREEM (H.), Practical Astronomy, (Orr's Circle of the Sciences).

BUTLER (A.), Lives of the Saints.

BUTLER (S.), Modern and Ancient Geography.

EWALD, Geschichte des Volks Israel bis Christus.

FELLER, Dictionnaire Historique.

GESENIUS, Hebräisches Lexikon.

GOERRES (J.), Christliche Mystik.

HIND (J. H.), Solar System.

HÖFLER, Deutschen Päpste.

KARCHER (Dr), Schulwörterbuch der Lateinischen Sprache in Etymologischer Ordnung.

M'CABE, Catholic History of England.

MANUAL of Church History. Burns and Lambert.

MOLITOR, Philosophie der Geschichte.

NEANDER (Dr), Life of Christ.

NEWMAN (J. H.), Development of Christian Doctrine.

PASSOW, Handwörterbuch der Griechischen Sprache.

PATTERSON, Journal of a Tour in Egypt, &c.

PITRA (Dom.), Etudes sur les Actes des Saints.

SEPP (Dr), Leben Christi.

TENNEMAN (T.), Manual of the History of Philosophy.

ANCIENT HISTORY.

B.C.
4004.—Creation, according to the Hebrew Text.
4700.—Creation, according to the Samaritan Pentateuch.
5872.—Creation, according to the Septuagint Version.

CHAPTER I.

THE earth, the sun, the moon, the stars, and all that forms the universe,[1] have had a beginning. These creatures owe their existence to a Supreme[2] Being, Himself existing[3] from all eternity; having therefore neither beginning nor end. He made all things out of nothing by a mere act of His will; therefore His attributes[4] of power and of perfection exceed[5] the comprehension[6] of man. This perfect Being we call God.

Because of His perfection,[7] God is not subject[8] to the imperfections which we see in everything material.

Matter[9] is limited, inert,[10] unintelligent,[11] divisible, and subject to decay.

[1] *Unus*, one; *versor*, of which one meaning is, to be. In Greek, *To Pan*, The All.

[2] *Supremus*, highest, from *super*, above.

[3] Prefix, *Ex*, out; *sisto*, I stand.

[4] Prefix *ad*, to; *tribuo*, I give, I hand over. Attribute signifies what we can say particularly belongs to any one.

[5] *Ex*, out of; *cedo*, I go. Synonym—to go beyond.

[6] *Com*, together; *prehendo* I take up. Syn.—to grasp.

[7] Prefix *per*, thoroughly; *factus*, done. Syn. of perfection—fulness. The fulness of the Godhead means the perfection of God.

[8] *Subjicio*, I put under. Syn.—liable to.

[9] Matter. Syn.—stuff.

[10] *In*, not; *ars*, art. Without art, form, or activity.

[11] *Un*, not; *inter*, within; *lego*, I gather; in such phrases as, I could not gather his meaning.

God is a Spirit whose intelligence is infinite, whose activity is without limit, whose omniscience[1] penetrates[2] the past, the present, and the future, and whose complete[3] unity excludes[4] all idea[5] of parts, of divisibility, or of finality.[6]

Yet in God there are three persons—the Father, the Son, and the Holy Ghost ; so that there is trinity of persons and unity of nature. This is the mystery[7] of the Holy Trinity.

In order to give some idea of this mystery, God the Father has been represented as a venerable old man—as a type[8] of eternity. God the Son appears more youthful, on account of his title, although He is eternal as the Father. God the Holy Ghost is represented as a dove, because He manifested[9] Himself in this form. We must remember that these figures are only allegorical.[10] The Son of God is also named "The Word ;" as St John says, "In the beginning was the Word, and the Word was with God, and the Word was God." (John i. 1.)

Another symbol[11] used to represent the Holy Trinity is an equilateral triangle.[12] This is intended[13] to shew that the three persons are co-equal, and form one whole.

God having existed from all eternity, and no other being having co-existed with Him, it pleased Him to create the heaven and the earth, and all that is therein ; and thus to make manifest His wisdom and His power.

He first created out of nothing the material of which He intended to compose the universe, and those creatures He destined to govern it under His supreme sovereignty ; and, in order to shew that this creation was not the effect of any

[1] *Omnis*, all ; *scio*, I know. Syn.—all-knowing.
[2] Penetrates, pierces. Celtic, *pen*, a point or top.
[3] *Con*, together ; *pleo*, I fill. Syn.—full.
[4] *Ex*, out of ; *claudo*, I shut. Syn.—shuts out.
[5] Idea, a Greek word for image, or picture in the mind.
[6] *Finis*, end ; *finality*, ending.
[7] Mystery, Greek, *muo, muso*, to shut ; *mueo*, to irritate.
[8] Type, from a Greek word meaning figure.
[9] Manifested, made plain. Etymology uncertain. Latin, *manifestus ;* Celtic, *meanan*, plain.
[10] Allegorical, figuratively descriptive of *real* parts, from the Greek, *allos*, another ; *agoreuo*, to speak.
[11] Symbol, the sign of a moral thing by the image of a natural thing, from Greek *sun*, together, *ballo*, to throw, to compare.
[12] A figure in geometry shut in by three equal lines, thus △.
[13] *In*, against ; *tendo*, I stretch. Syn.—meant.

necessary cause, but the production[1] of a voluntary[2] act, God gave to this work successive[3] degrees[4] of perfection in an admirable[5] order.

CHAPTER II.

THE first day God made the light, that fluid[6] which is everywhere diffused,[7] and is probably the same as heat. It is thought that on this day God created the angels—celestial[8] spirits who serve God in making known and in executing[9] His will.

The second day God created the firmament,[10] and divided the waters which were under the firmament from the waters which were above the firmament; and to each fluid He gave the density[11] requisite[12] to form that harmonious[13] balance established by God for the general good. And God called the firmament heaven.

The third day God separated[14] the waters from the dry land, gathering the former into those great basins called seas, and raising up the dry land, which God called earth. On this day were also produced all plants bearing seed which cover and embellish[15] this terrestrial[16] globe, from the cedar to the hyssop, from the cactus to the violet.

The fourth day God made the sun, the moon, and the stars, to give light and heat to the seeds and the plants, as well as to serve as a salutary[17] influence[18] to more perfect creatures, and to celestial beings.

The fifth day the waters brought forth abundantly every kind of fish, and the air was peopled with birds—living creatures, which not only vegetate[19] like plants, but have, moreover,

---

[1] *Pro*, before; *duco*, I lead. Syn.—bringing forth.
[2] Voluntary, with free will.
[3] *Sub*, under; *cedo*, I go. Signifies, one after the other.
[4] From *gradus*, a step.   [5] *Ad*, to; *miro*, I look. Syn.—wonderful.
[6] *Fluo*, I flow. Anything not solid.
[7] Prefix *dis*, asunder; *fundo*, I pour. Syn.—spread.
[8] Celestial. Syn.—Heavenly, from *cælum*, heaven.
[9] *Ex*, out of; *sequor*, I follow up. Syn.—to carry out.
[10] Hebrew, expanse.   [11] *Densus*, thick. Syn.—thickness.
[12] *Re*, back; *quæro*, I seek. Syn.—sought.
[13] *Harmonia*, Greek, a fitting together—a term in music.
[14] *Se*, different; *paro*, part. Syn.—cut off.
[15] Embellish. Syn.—beautify.   [16] From *terra*, the earth, meaning earthly.
[17] Salutary, from *salus*, health. Syn.—health-giving.
[18] From *in*, to: and *fluo*, to flow.   [19] Vegetate. Syn.—to grow.

the faculty[1] of movement, and which swim or fly according to the element to which they belong.

The sixth day were created the animals destined to people the earth, and to serve the chief to whom God was to give dominion[2] over them. This chief was man, of whom it is said that God created him to His own image; that is, he not only received a body like the lower animals, but also a soul, in which he was like unto God—having the faculty to perceive[3] and to will, to know and to love. Thus, man being endowed with intelligence and free-will, is left at liberty to choose between a good or a bad use of these faculties, and he is either acceptable to God or culpable[4] in His sight, according to the choice he makes between good or evil.

The first man was called Adam,[5] and the first woman Eve.[6] God gave her to be a companion unto Adam, and their union was the origin of marriage.

The seventh day God rested from all His work which He had made; and God blessed the seventh day, and sanctified it, and ordained that it should be kept holy. Therefore, on the Sabbath-day,[7] man is to rest from his labours, and to meditate upon the works of God,—to adore Him, and thus to prepare himself for that eternal repose for which God has destined him.

Unhappily, Adam and Eve made a bad use of the privileges[8] which God had bestowed upon them. They had been placed in the garden of Eden,[9] which the Lord God had planted, and in which He had made to grow every tree that was pleasant to the sight and good for food; especially the tree of life, the fruit of which preserved them in health and strength.

Adam and Eve were destined to dress and to keep this earthly paradise;[10] this happy lot was to be theirs until the time when God should transport them to heaven, there to enjoy, in His celestial paradise, the infinite happiness of complete union with God.

[1] Faculty. Syn.—power.
[2] *Dominus*, Lord. Syn.—lordship.
[3] Prefix *per*, thoroughly; *capio*, I take. Syn.—to take in.
[4] Culpable, from *culpa*, a fault. Syn.—guilty.
[5] The name Adam means Man, or Red Man.
[6] Eve means Life.
[7] Sabbath means rest.
[8] Privilege. *Privus*, separate; *lex*, a law. Peculiar advantage.
[9] Eden means Delight, or Pleasure.
[10] Paradise means a park or garden.

But God wished to teach these rational[1] and free beings that He had given them far higher capacities[2] than those for mere material enjoyment, and that gratitude[3] and obedience to Him for so many benefits[4] would complete their own happiness as well as the glory of God. In order, therefore, to try their love and obedience, God commanded them *not* to eat of one tree, which *grew in the* midst of the garden of Eden. This was the tree of the knowledge of good and evil. Of every other tree they might freely eat.

This slight privation did not disturb[5] their happiness. Their obedience would have been meritorious—their disobedience would be punished; for God had said, "Of the tree of knowledge of good and evil, thou shalt not eat: for in what day soever thou shalt eat of it, thou shalt die the death." (Gen. ii. 17.)

CHAPTER III.

Now, one of those angels created by God to serve Him, but who had incurred[6] the wrath of his Creator for the sin of pride, and had, with other rebellious angels, been precipitated[7] into hell, became envious of the happiness and the innocence[8] of Adam and Eve, as well as of the many favours and the love which God had conferred[9] upon them. This fallen angel, called the devil,[10] undertook to make our first parents rebellious,[11] and thus to bring about the fall of man by disobedience, as he and the rebel angels had fallen by pride. The devil took the form of a serpent, and tempted Eve to eat of the forbidden fruit; she gave also unto her husband, and he did eat.

[1] From *ratio*, reason. Syn.—reasonable.
[2] From *capax*, roomy, or holding. Syn.—grasp, or power.
[3] *Gratus*, thankful. Syn.—thankfulness.
[4] From *bene*, well; and *facio*, I do. Syn.—good deeds, or well-doing.
[5] Prefix *dis*, a part; and *turbo*, to trouble. Syn.—break up, or trouble.
[6] Prefix *in*, against; *curro*, I run. Syn.—dared.
[7] From *præceps*, headlong; meaning tumbled headlong.
[8] *In*, not; *noceo*, I hurt. Syn.—harmless.
[9] Prefix *con*, together; *fero*, I bear.
[10] διαβαλλω, I pierce through—slander; διαβολον, devil. The word devil is connected with the Persian *div*, angel, and the Latin *deus*, God.
[11] Prefix *re* again; and *bellum*, war.

Their disobedience was soon punished. God first cursed the devil who, under the form of a serpent, had beguiled Eve, but promised[1] a Saviour to redeem[2] man from his power, and to bruise his head. Then God sentenced Adam and Eve to suffering and to death, and said, "Cursed is the earth in thy work; with labour and toil shalt thou eat thereof all the days of thy life. In the sweat of thy face shalt thou eat bread, till thou return to the earth, out of which thou wast taken : for dust thou art, and unto dust thou shalt return." (Gen. iii. 17, 19.)

The sin of Adam was not only punished in a material sense, but the soul of man also underwent a terrible[3] change. Instead of being adorned with intelligence and goodness, he became alienated[4] from God, and subject to every evil inclination.[5] Thus, having forfeited[6] God's favour, he became liable to eternal punishment in hell with the devil and his angels.

This sad inheritance of suffering and death was handed down by Adam to his posterity;[7] but God in His mercy did not leave the human race without hope. Adam and Eve were permitted[8] to know that their sin would be repaired, and that their repentance would be accepted[9] through the merits of the coming Redeemer; and He was to crush the serpent's head, as God had announced[10] to them.

Thus Adam lost paradise, and was driven forth to till the ground from whence he was taken ; and God placed cherubim, and a flaming sword which turned every way, to keep the way of the tree of life, lest man should eat of it and live for ever.

CHAPTER IV.

CAIN[11] was the eldest son of Adam and Eve, and the first born of all men. Abel[12] was their second son ; and Abel was a keeper of sheep, but Cain was a tiller of the ground. Both

---

[1] *Pro*, before ; *mitto*, I send.   [2] *Re*, back ; *emo*, I buy.
[3] Terrible, from *terror*, fright. Meaning of terrible, fear-inspiring.

offered[1] sacrifices[2] unto the Lord. Cain brought of the fruit of the ground, and Abel the firstlings of his flock; and the Lord accepted Abel and his offering, but unto Cain and his offering He had not respect.

And Cain was very angry, and his countenance fell; and God reproved Cain, and said, "Why art thou wroth? If thou do well, shalt thou not receive?" But Cain was jealous of his brother, and instead of trying to please God, and thus to make his sacrifice acceptable to Him, Cain rose up against Abel, and slew his brother. Even then, if he had repented, and had not despaired of God's mercy, he would have been forgiven; but he continued obstinate.[3] Then the curse of God fell upon him, and he was driven forth a fugitive[4] on the earth.

And God gave another son to Adam, and Eve named him Seth,[5] to console them for the loss of Abel; and Adam was 130 years old when Seth was born.

When Seth was 105 years old he had a son named Enos;[6] and Seth lived 912 years, and his son Enos 905 years. The [divine] worship[7] of God was established by Enos;[8] and the descendants[9] of Seth were called the children of God, but the descendants of Cain were called the children of men.

When Enos was ninety years old, his son Cainan[10] was born; and Cainan lived to be 910 years old.

Malaleel,[11] (Ma-la'le-el,) his son, was born A.M. 395; lived 395 years.

Jared,[12] the son of Malaleel, was born A.M. 1422, and he lived 962 years.

Henoch, his son, did not stay long on earth; for God took him up to heaven without his having undergone the penalty of death, when he was only 365 years old.

Mathusala, (Ma-thu'sa-la,) his son, was 300 years old when Henoch was taken up into heaven. He lived longer than any

[1] *Ob*, against; *fero*, I carry.   [2] *Sacrum*, holy; *facio*, I make.
[3] *Ob*, against; *sisto*, I stand. Syn.—stubborn.   [4] *Fugio*, I fly.
[5] Seth means Germ, or Child; some say, Foundation of the world.
[6] Enos means Man.
[7] Worship, from worth and ship, state of being worthy.
[8] In Scripture names of *two syllables*, the accent is always on the first syllable, as E'nos, Ja'red.
[9] *De*, from; *scando*, I come.   [10] Cainan means the same as Cain.
[11] Malaleel, or Mahalal-el, means the God of Splendour.
[12] Jared means River.

of the patriarchs,[1] and died the year of the deluge, when he was 969 years old. God sometimes begins to recompense[2] His elect even upon earth.

Lamech,[3] son to Mathusala, was 182 years old before Noe was born to him.

The prayers and sacrifices Lamech offered to God in behalf of his son Noe, preserved him from the contagion of sin which had spread abroad upon the earth.

The race of Cain had also multiplied. He had built a city, and called it after his son Henoch ;[4] and in it he established his children.

The descendants of Henoch, Jubal and Tubalcain,[5] were the • inventors[6] of many useful arts, and of musical[7] instruments.[8] But they neglected the virtues which alone form the happiness and the perfection of the soul.

CHAPTER V.

ADAM was 930 years old when he died. He had seen the wickedness of his posterity, and deeply repented his own sin, which had brought death and corruption[9] into the world.

The descendants of Seth had intermarried with the posterity of Cain ; and the wickedness of the world was so great, that God said he would destroy[10] the earth and the whole human race.

But Noe,[11] the son of Lamech, found grace in the eyes of the Lord ; for he was a just man, and perfect in his generation.[12]

Then the Lord announced unto Noe that He intended to

---

[1] Patriarchs. *Patria*, Greek, a family ; *archos*, a chief.
[2] *Re*, back ; *con*, together ; *pendo*, I weigh or pay. Syn.—reward.
[3] Lamech means a Wild Man, or robber.—*Ewald.*
[4] Henoch signifies the Beginner, the initiating.—*Gesenius.*
[5] Jubal and Tubal mean Sons, or children ; literally fruit, production.
[6] *In*, into ; *venio*, I come.
[7] From *musa*, a muse. The Muses were the goddesses of art among the Greeks and Romans. One of them was thought to be the author of harmony.
[8] *In*, into ; *struo*, I build. Syn.—tools.
[9] *Co*, together ; *rumpo*, I break. Means spoiling, breaking up, ruin.
[10] *De*, from ; and *struo*, I build. Syn.—break up.
[11] Noah means Fresh, new. Others say it means Rest ; also, the Comforter.
[12] *Genus*, a race, generation. Means here, age ; those who lived at the same time.

bring a flood of waters upon the earth, and to destroy all flesh; and Noe was commanded to build an ark, as a refuge[1] for himself and his family during the flood.

The ark was finished A.M. 1656.

Noe was 600 years old when the flood of waters was upon the earth.

And Noe went in, and his sons, and his wife, and his sons' wives, in all eight persons, into the ark.

And of every living thing of all flesh, of beasts and of fowls, and of everything that creepeth upon the earth, there went in two and two into the ark, as God had commanded Noe.

Then the rain began to fall, and the fountains of the great deep were broken up, and the windows of heaven were opened.

And the flood was forty days and forty nights upon the earth, and the highest mountains were covered; and Noe only remained[2] alive, and they that were with him in the ark.

And the waters prevailed[3] upon the earth an hundred and fifty days.

The waters then began to abate[4] during another one hundred and fifty days, and Noe sent forth a raven and a dove. The raven did not return, but the dove returned. Seven days after he sent her forth again, and she returned with an olive-leaf in her mouth. Noe sent forth the dove again seven days after, and she returned no more. The ark soon after rested on one of the mountains of Ararat in Armenia;[5] and Noe and his family, and all that were with him, left the ark, after having passed one year in it.

[1] *Re*, back; *fugo*, I fly. A shelter.
[2] *Re*, back; *maneo*, I stay.
[3] *Prae*, before; *valere*, strong. Signifies to have the upper hand.
[4] Abate, lessen.
[5] Armenia was divided by the ancients into Great and Little Armenia. The former was separated from the latter by the Euphrates. The principal rivers of Armenia were the Euphrates, the Tigris, and the Araxes. Artaxata, on the Araxes, was for a long time its capital.

PERIOD II., OR TIME IMMEDIATELY SUCCEEDING THE DELUGE,
427 YEARS.   FROM B.C. 2348 TO 1921.

SCRIPTURE HISTORY. B.C.	AFRICA.	ASIA.	EUROPE.
2348. The Deluge ends. 2247. Babel. 1996. Birth of Abraham.	The family of Ham or Cham were the progenitors of Africans, Arabians, and Cananites. B.C. 2188. Mizraim or Menes founds the kingdom of Egypt.	The family of Sem were the progenitors of the nations of Asia. B.C. 2050. Kingdom of Assyria begins.	Greece and Europe supposed to have been peopled by Japheth. In Scripture, Greece and its islands are called " The isles of the Gentiles." B.C. 2089. Sicyon founded.

CHAPTER VI.

THE first act of Noe was to build an altar,[1] and to offer burnt-offerings unto God ; and the Lord said in His heart, I will not again curse the earth any more for man's sake ; neither will I again smite everything living, as I have done.

And God promised that seedtime and harvest, summer and winter, and day and night should not cease ; and He blessed Noe and his posterity, and made a covenant[2] with him not to destroy the earth any more by a flood, and the rainbow was to be an everlasting sign of this promise.

After the flood, Noe began to be an husbandman, and he planted a vineyard, and drinking of the wine, he was made drunk ; and his son Cham[3] mocked his father.   When Noe awoke from his wine, and knew what his younger son had done, he foretold that the descendants of Cham should be servants to the descendants of Sem[4] and Japheth ;[5] but them he blessed, because they were dutiful.

And men had again multiplied upon the earth, and all were of one language[6] and of one speech ; and as they journeyed from the east they found a plain in the land of Sennaar, and they dwelt there.

And they said one to another, "Come, let us make a city and a tower, the top whereof may reach to heaven ; and let us make our name famous, before we be scattered abroad into all lands."

[1] Altar.   Altus, high ; ara, altar.
[2] Covenant.   Con and venio, a coming together, agreement.
[3] Cham or Ham is thought to mean Hot, or Heated.
[4] Sem signifies Name, or Fame.
[5] Japheth is said to mean a Wanderer, or the Spreading.

But God wished them to be dispersed. He therefore confounded[1] their language, so that they no longer understood each other; and the name of the place was called Babel.[2] Then they left off building the city and the tower, and the Lord scattered them abroad upon the face of all the earth.

The descendants of Japheth peopled Europe; those of Sem settled in Asia; and the posterity of Ham, with a few exceptions,[3] peopled Africa.

This dispersion took place towards the middle of the eighteenth century after the creation, and Noah lived after the flood 350 years; and all the days of Noah were 950 years, and he died in the year 2006. And Abraham[4] was born two years after Noe's death, A.M. 2008.

At this period profane[5] history begins to leave us a few traditions, such as the foundation of Sicyon, (Si"cyon,) which claimed to be the oldest town in Greece. The earliest kingdoms of Babylon, Assyria, and Egypt were also founded; but of their history we have no very reliable knowledge.

PERIOD III., OR PATRIARCHAL PERIOD, 430 YEARS.
FROM B.C. 1921 TO 1491.

SCRIPTURE HISTORY.	AFRICA.	ASIA.	EUROPE.
B.C.	B.C.		B.C.
1921. Call of Abraham.	1827. Shepherd kings.		1856. Argos built.
1896. Birth of Isaac.	1724. The dynasty ends.		1556. Athens founded by Cecrops.
1706. Jacob removes into Egypt.			1516. Sparta founded by Lelex.
1571. Birth of Moses.			1493. Thebes founded by Cadmus.
1491. The Exodus.			

CHAPTER VII.

As the descendants of Noe increased[6] and were dispersed over the earth, they gradually forsook the worship of the only true God. They began to adore[7] the sun, the moon, and men

---

[1] *Con*, together; *fundo*, I pour.   [2] Babel means Mixture, Confusion.

[3] *Ex*, out of; *capio*, I take.

[4] Abraham means the Father of a multitude.

[5] *Pro*, before, outside; *fanum*, the temple.   [6] *In*, into; *cresco*, I grow.

[7] *Ad*, to; *ora*, the mouth. Putting the hand to the mouth is still a sign of respect and salutation of superiors in the East.

like to themselves, and animals, and even statues of gold and of silver, of wood and of stone. They thus became idolaters,[1] or worshippers of false gods. We find in the Bible, as well as in other histories, a sad picture of the almost general corruption into which mankind had again fallen, owing to their wilful forgetfulness of God.

There were still a few amongst the people who continued to serve God; and the Bible makes mention of Melchisedech,[2] (Mel-chis'e-dech,) king of Salem,[3] who was a priest of the most high God.

In order to preserve[4] the traditions[5] of the true religion, which, humanly speaking, might be lost, God resolved to choose a people and a country to keep the ancient revelations, and to teach by a visible[6] authority the commands which God intended to give them.

Mathusala, the grandfather of Noe, died the year of the deluge, and was 969 years old when he died. He had lived 300 years with Adam, and had heard from the lips of the father of mankind all the primitive traditions. These, Methusala taught again to Noe, and to Noe's son Sem; and Sem lived 600 years, and he died.

Abraham descended from Sem, and lived with Thare,[7] his father, in Ur of the Chaldees,[8] (Chal-dæ'a.) And Thare took Abraham, and Sarah,[9] Abraham's wife, and Lot,[10] the son of Haran, his son's son; and they went forth from Ur of the Chaldees, and they came unto Haran in Mesopotamia,[11] (Mes-o-po-ta'mi-a,) and dwelt there: and Thare died at Haran.

Now the Lord said unto Abraham, "Go forth out of thy country, and out of thy father's house, and come into a land which I will shew thee.

"And I will make of thee a great nation, and I will bless thee; and in thee shall all the kindreds of the earth be blessed."

So Abraham departed, and Lot, his nephew, went with him,

---

[1] *Idos*, object, picture; *latria*, service.
[2] Melchisedech, King of Justice.   [3] Salem, Peace, or Reward.
[4] *Pre*, before; *servo*, I keep.   [5] *Trado*, I hand. I hand down.
[6] Visible, that can be seen.   [7] Thare, or Terah, means to wander.
[8] Ur of the Chaldees, an idolatrous country.
[9] Sarah means Lady, or Princess.
[10] Lot, a covering.
[11] Mesopotamia, between the rivers Tigris and Euphrates.

and Sarah, Abraham's wife; and they came unto Bethel,[1] in the land of Canaan, now called Palestine.[2] Abraham was at this time seventy-five years old.

CHAPTER VIII.

LOT, his nephew, had parted from Abraham because their herdsmen could not agree, and had settled near Sodom,[3] the inhabitants of which, as well as those of Gomorrha, (Go-mor'ra,) were exceedingly wicked; and there came two angels to Sodom, and Lot prayed them to stay with him, and to refresh themselves with food and rest. Then the men of Sodom insulted these strangers, whom they knew not to be angels, and the angels struck them with blindness.

Lot was ordered by the angels to leave the city, with his wife and his two daughters, and they were commanded by them not to look back during their flight; but curiosity to see what was to take place induced Lot's wife to look behind her, and she was changed into a pillar of salt as a punishment for her disobedience. Then the Lord rained brimstone and fire out of heaven, and utterly destroyed the cities of the plain; and the site of them to this day is covered by a pestilential lake, called the Dead Sea.[4]

When Abraham was an hundred years old, his wife Sarah gave birth to Isaac,[5] called the Child of Promise, because in him and his posterity were the Divine promises to be fulfilled.

And it came to pass that, as God wished to put Abraham's faith and obedience to the proof, he was told by God to take his only-beloved son into the land of Moriah, and to offer him there for a burnt-offering upon one of the mountains, which was to be shewn him.

---

[1] Bethel, house or place of God; Bethlehem, house of bread.
[2] Palestine, so called from its ancient inhabitants the Philistines.
[3] Sodom, Desolate.
[4] This lake is more than 1100 feet below the level of the Mediterranean, and though it has no outlet, and receives the fresh waters of the Jordan and other rivers, yet its bitterness remains unchanged. Persons who have bathed in it say that the waters are so buoyant it is difficult to keep the feet under in swimming; and so salt, that it makes the eyes and the nose smart very unpleasantly. The ground for more than a mile round this lake is encrusted with salt.—*Journal of a Tour in Egypt, Palestine, Syria, and Greece. By J. L. Patterson, M.A.* 1852.   [5] Isaac, (Heb.,) meaning Laughter.

And Abraham rose up early, and took two of his young men and Isaac, and went unto the place of which God had told him.

Then, on the third day, Abraham saw the place afar off; and he said unto his young men, "Stay you here, and I and the lad will go yonder and worship."

And Abraham took the wood for the burnt-offering, and laid it upon Isaac his son; and he took the fire in his hand, and a knife; and they went both of them together.

And Isaac said, "My father, behold the fire and the wood; but where is the victim for the holocaust?"[1]

And Abraham said, "God will provide Himself a victim for an holocaust."

And they came to the place which God had shewn him; and Abraham built an altar, and laid the wood in order, and bound Isaac his son, and laid him on the altar upon the wood.

And Abraham took the knife to slay his son, and the angel of the Lord called unto him out of heaven, and said, "Lay not thy hand upon the lad; for now I know that thou fearest God, seeing thou hast not spared thy only-begotten son for my sake."

And God again blessed Abraham and his posterity for ever.

CHAPTER IX.

ISAAC married Rebecca,[2] granddaughter of Nachor, Abraham's brother; and he had two sons, Esau and Jacob. And Esau,[3] the elder, sold his birthright to his brother Jacob[4] for a mess of pottage; and, consequently,[5] all the blessings which were to have been Esau's fell to Jacob. And Esau hated Jacob because he had defrauded him of his father Isaac's blessing; and Jacob was obliged to fly, in order to escape the anger of his brother Esau.

Then Jacob went to Haran, in Mesopotamia, where his uncle Laban dwelt; and during his journey, he had a vision, in which he beheld a ladder, and the top of it reached to heaven, with the angels of God ascending[6] and descending on it. God himself stood above it, and renewed to Jacob the promises already made

---

[1] Holocaust. Greek, *holos*, whole; *kaustos*, burnt. Syn.—whole burnt-offering.

[2] A noosed cord.   [3] Esau means Hairy. Surnamed Edom, red.

to Abraham. Jacob lived twenty years near his uncle Laban, and married Lia and Rachel, Laban's daughters. He then returned to Canaan, and was reconciled to his brother Esau.

Jacob had eleven sons, and Ruben, Simeon, Levi, and Juda were the four eldest; but Joseph[1] was the youngest of the eleven. Now Israel loved Joseph more than all his children, because he was the son of his old age; and fifteen years later, Rachel had another son, called Benjamin,[2] and she died.

And Joseph dreamed a dream, and he said unto his brethren, "Hear, I pray you, this dream : ' Behold, we were binding sheaves in the field ; and, lo, my sheaf arose, and also stood upright, and, behold, your sheaves stood round about, and bowed down to my sheaf.'"

And his brethren said, "Shalt thou be our king ?" And they hated him for his dreams, and for his words.

And Joseph dreamed yet another dream, and told it his brethren : "Behold, the sun, and the moon, and the eleven stars worshipped me." ·

And his brethren envied him because of his dreams, and because of the exceeding love his father bore him.

And his brethren went to feed their father's flocks in Sichem.

And Israel said to Joseph, "Go, I pray thee, see whether it be well with thy brethren, and with the flocks, and bring me word again."

And Joseph sought his brethren. And when they saw him afar off, they said, "Behold, this dreamer cometh ;" and they conspired[3] against him to slay him.

But Ruben, the elder, who did not wish them to hurt the lad, said, "Shed no blood, but cast him into this empty pit." And when they had done this, Ruben left them to plan some other means of getting Joseph safely back to his father. But whilst he was away, Joseph's brethren saw a company of Madianite[4] merchants[5] going into Egypt, and Juda proposed[6] to sell Joseph to them instead of killing him. To this they all

---

[1] Joseph. Gesenius says the name may come from the verb, " He is carried away."

[2] Son of the right hand, or happy.   [3] *Con*, together; *spiro*, I breathe.

[4] Madianite, descendant of Madian, the third son of Japheth. Hence, probably, the Medes.

[5] *Mercor*, I buy.   [6] *Pro*, before ; *pono*, I place.

agreed; so they drew Joseph out of the pit, and sold him to the merchants for twenty pieces of silver.

And Ruben returned to the pit, and behold Joseph was not there; and he rent his clothes for grief.

Then the brethren took Joseph's coat of many colours, and dipped it in the blood of a goat, and sent it to their father; and Jacob knew it, and said, "It is my son's coat; an evil beast hath devoured[1] him."

And Jacob rent his clothes, and put on sackcloth, and mourned for his son many days.

All his sons and his daughters rose up to comfort him, but he refused to be comforted; and he said, "I will go down into the grave unto my son mourning." Thus his father wept for Joseph.

CHAPTER X.

The Ismaelites[2] who had bought Joseph took him into Egypt, and sold him to Putiphar, (Put'-i-phar,) an Egyptian of high rank in the court of Pharao,[3] king of Egypt.

And the Lord was with Joseph, and made all that he did to prosper in his hand.

And his master saw that the Lord was with him, and Joseph found grace in his sight; and Putiphar made him overseer over all that he had, and the Lord blessed the Egyptian's house for Joseph's sake.

But it came to pass that Putiphar's wife accused[4] Joseph falsely of a very great crime, and Putiphar believed her; and his wrath was kindled against Joseph, and he had him cast into prison.

But the Lord was with Joseph, and gave him favour in the sight of the keeper of the prison, who committed[5] the direction[6] of all the other prisoners into Joseph's hand.

Amongst these prisoners were the king of Egypt's chief butler and his chief baker, who had offended[7] their lord, and

---

[1] *De*, from; *voro*, I swallow.

[2] Ismaelite, descendant of Ismael, son of Abraham, but not the son of promise. From him are descended the Arabs.

[3] Pharao is not a proper name, it means the King, *pe-a-ro*—He is the king.

[4] *Ad*, to; *causa*, a case.   [5] *Con*, together; *mitto*, I send.

[6] *Dia*, through; *rectus*, straight.   [7] *Ob*, against; *fendo*, I thrust, or parry.

had been put into the prison where Joseph was, and Joseph had charge of them.

They both of them dreamed prophetically, and Joseph gave them the interpretation[1] of their dreams ; and everything came to pass as he said it would : the chief butler was taken again into favour, and the chief baker was hanged.

It happened that, at the end of two full years, Pharao, king of Egypt, had a dream, which none of his magicians[2] or wise men could interpret. Then the chief butler remembered Joseph ; and Pharao, hearing what he had done for his chief butler and his chief baker, sent for him out of prison, and he interpreted Pharao's dream.

The dream of Pharao was of a great famine,[3] which was to afflict Egypt and the neighbouring countries during seven years, and of seven years of plenty which were to precede the famine.

And Pharao said unto Joseph, "Forasmuch as God has shewed thee all this, there is none so discreet[4] and wise as thou art. I will make thee ruler over all the land of Egypt."

And Joseph was thirty years old when he became governor of Egypt. And Pharao gave him to wife the daughter of Putiphare, priest of Heliopolis ;[5] and unto Joseph were born two sons, Manasses and Ephraim.

CHAPTER XI.

THE seven years of plenty had passed away, and the seven years of dearth began to be felt; but in all the land of Egypt there was bread, because of the great storehouses which Joseph had stored during the years of plenty : and all countries came into Egypt to buy corn of Joseph.

The famine was sorely felt in the land of Canaan, where Jacob and his sons dwelt. And he said unto them, "I hear there is corn in Egypt. Go you down thither, and buy, that we may live and not die."

Then ten of the sons of Israel came to Joseph, and bowed down to him; and Joseph knew his brethren, though they

---

[1] *Interpres,* an explainer. [2] *Magia,* sorcery, witchcraft. [3] *Fames,* hunger.
[4] *Dis,* apart; *cerno,* I observe. Discreet means prudent.
[5] Heliopolis, City of the Sun; called also On and Beth-shemesh. (Jer. xliii. 13.)

knew not Joseph.   But Joseph, wishing to try them, pretended[1]
to think them spies, and put them in prison during three days.
He then let them go, under promise of returning with their
youngest brother, Benjamin, into Egypt.

Jacob was very grieved to part from his son, but the famine
was very sore; he was therefore obliged[2] to send his sons, and
his beloved son Benjamin with them, once more into Egypt.

When Joseph saw his young brother, he wept, and said unto
his brethren, "I am Joseph: does my father yet live?"   And
his brethren could not answer, for they were troubled at his
presence.[3]   But Joseph said, "Be not grieved nor angry with
yourselves that ye sold me hither, for God did send me before
you to preserve life; haste ye, and bring down my father
hither."   And he fell upon his brother Benjamin's neck, and
Benjamin wept on his neck.

So Joseph sent his brethren away, and they departed, and
came into the land of Canaan, unto Jacob their father, and
told him, "Joseph is yet alive; and he is governor over all the
land of Egypt."   And Jacob's heart fainted, for he believed
them not.   But when he saw the waggons Joseph had sent to
carry him, the spirit of Jacob revived,[4] and Israel said, "It is
enough; Joseph my son is yet alive: I will go and see him
before I die."

And Jacob took his journey with all that he had—his sons
and his sons' sons, his daughter and his sons' daughters, their
cattle and their goods—and came into Egypt.   And Joseph
presented his father to Pharao; and Jacob was settled with
his family in the land of Gessen.   This was in the year B.C.
1706, and 215 years after the covenant with Abraham.

Jacob (also called Israel) lived seventeen years in the land of
Egypt.   And Joseph buried him with his fathers in the land of
Canaan—with Abraham and Sarah his wife, and with Isaac
and Rebecca his wife.

[1] *Præ*, before; *tendo*, I stretch.
[2] *Ob*, against; *ligo*, I bind.
[3] *Pre*, before; *sentio*, I feel.
[4] *Re*, again; *vivus*, alive.

CHAPTER XII.

ABOUT one hundred and twenty years after Jacob's death the Israelites, or Hebrews, had multiplied so greatly, that the Egyptians began to fear their numbers; and Pharao - Rameses, (Pha-ra-o-Ra-me'-ses,) the king, treated them like slaves, and even tried to destroy their race, by having all the male Israelites drowned in the river Nile.

A child of the tribe of Levi, called Moses,[1] was thus exposed[2] in a little ark of bulrushes. And the daughter of Pharao came down to bathe in the river; she took compassion on the child, and had him brought up in her own palace, where he was instructed in all the learning of the Egyptians.

When he was forty years old he saw an Egyptian smiting a Hebrew; and he slew the Egyptian, and was obliged to fly from Pharao into the land of Madian, (Ma'-di-an), on the opposite[3] side of the Red Sea. And he dwelt there; and married a daughter of Jethro, the priest[4] of Madian, and kept the flock of his father-in-law.

One day on Mount Horeb[5] he saw a bush on fire, and the bush was not consumed.[6] And Moses turned aside to see why the bush was not burned.

And God called unto him out of the bush, and ordered him to return into Egypt, to be the liberator[7] of his people.

Moses and Aaron[8] his brother went to Pharao-Amenophis, (Pha-ra-o-A-me'-no-phis,) and asked, in the name of God, that the Israelites might go to offer sacrifices in the desert.

But Pharao refused to let Israel go, and would not hearken unto Moses.

Then God sent many plagues on Egypt. The rivers and all the waters were changed into blood: then myriads[9] of frogs covered the land, and all the dust of the land throughout Egypt

[1] The name Moses is supposed to be of Egyptian origin, and to mean "saved from the water."—*Gesenius*. *Mou*, means water; *set*, saved, in Coptic.
[2] *Ex*, out of; *pono*, I place.
[3] *Ob*, against; *pono*, I place. Syn.—facing.
[4] Priest, from *presbuteros*, elder. Comparative of *presbus*, old.
[5] Horeb means, desolate.
[6] *Con*, together; *sumo*, I take.
[7] *Libero*, I free, I set free.
[8] Aaron, or Aharon.
[9] From *murios*, Greek for ten thousand. It also signifies an immense number.—*Passow's Greek Lexicon*.

became sciniphs ;[1] then swarms of flies were sent, followed by a grievous murrain[2] of beasts, and then a plague of boils and blains upon man and upon beast; after that, the Lord sent thunder and hail, and fire mingled[3] with the hail.

Then came locusts[4], and a plague of darkness which lasted for three days. But the last and most terrible of all these visitations[5] was the death of all the first-born throughout the land of Egypt. This gave rise to the Passover.[6] God ordered the Hebrews to kill a lamb in every household, and to take a bunch of hyssop, and dip it in the blood, and strike the lintel and the two side-posts of the houses with the blood of the flesh, which was to be roasted, and eaten with unleavened bread and bitter herbs.

CHAPTER XIII.

AND it came to pass that at midnight the Lord smote all the first-born of the land of Egypt, from the first-born of Pharao that sat on his throne, to the first-born of the captive[7] that was in the dungeon, and all the first-born of cattle. And there was a great cry in Egypt. But the destroying angel, when he saw the blood of the lamb on the lintel and on the side-posts of the doors, passed over those houses, and not one Hebrew child died. And God ordered the Israelites to keep the festival of the Passover, or sacrifice of the Paschal lamb, as an ordinance for ever.

Then the Egyptians and their king were in haste for the departure of the Israelites. And Pharao called Moses and Aaron in the night, and said, "Go, sacrifice to the Lord as you wish ; your sheep and herds take along with you." And the Egyptians pressed the Israelites to go forth out of the land, and gave them vessels of gold and of silver, and raiment.

---

[1] Sciniphs, or cinifs. Hebrew, *chinnim*. Small flying insects, very troublesome both to man and beast.

[2] Murrain, from *morior*. Sp., *morrina*.

[3] Syn.—to mix. From the Greek and Sanscrit *Misgo* and *Maks.*—*Eichoff, Vergleichung der Sprachen von Europa und Indien.*

[4] Locusts. Insects so called from their resemblance to (Lat.) *Locusta*, a cray-fish.

[5] *Visito*, from *video*, I see. Means, to look after. Hence, also, to call upon.

And the children of Israel went forth towards the Red Sea,[1] after having dwelt in Egypt four hundred and thirty years.

And Pharao's heart was again hardened, and he pursued the Israelites to destroy them. But Moses stretched out his hand over the sea, and the Lord caused the sea to go back by a strong east wind, and made the sea dry land, and the children of Israel passed over. And the Egyptians pursued,[2] and went in after them to the midst of the sea.

And the Lord said unto Moses, "Stretch out thine hand over the sea, that the waters may come again upon the Egyptians, upon their chariots, and upon their horsemen." And the Lord overthrew Pharao and all his army of the Egyptians in the midst of the sea, and Israel was saved.

About this time there lived in a neighbouring country to that into which the Hebrews had come, one of those who had kept the ancient traditions in his heart, and who was a model of patience[3] and of every virtue in the midst of great suffering and trial. The name of this holy man was Job.

The Exodus[4] of the children of Israel out of Egypt occurred B.C. 1491—215 years after Jacob had entered it, and, according to St Paul, 430 years after God's covenant with Abraham.

Fifty days after their departure out of Egypt, the children of Israel approached Mount Horeb, where Moses had received[5] the commands of God, to free His people; the other summit[6] was called Sinai.

The Israelites now formed a powerful people, who had no other laws than their own to follow; and henceforth the family of each of Jacob's sons took the name of tribe.

[1] The Red Sea, or Arabian Gulf, is separated from the Mediterranean Sea by the Isthmus of Suez. It divides Asia from Africa, and washes the coasts of Arabia, Egypt, and Abyssinia.

[2] Syn.—I follow.   [3] *Patior*, I suffer.

[4] *Ex*, out; *hodos*, a way, a journeying.

[5] *Re*, back or again; *capio*, to take. All the words derived from *capio* are spelt with the *e* before the *i*.

[6] *Summus*, highest. Syn. of summit—top.

PERIOD IV., OR TIME OF THE THEOCRACY,[1] 396 YEARS.
FROM B.C. 1491 TO 1095.

SCRIPTURE HISTORY.	AFRICA.	ASIA.	EUROPE.
B.C. 1491. The Exodus. The Pentateuch[2] written. 1445. Conquest of Palestine. 1405. The Judges begin. 1095. Theocracy ends by Samuel anointing[3] Saul king.	B.C. 1485. Ægyptus, or Rameses, or Sesostris.	B.C. 1406. Troy built. 1252. Tyre built. 1193. Siege of Troy. 1184. Troy taken.	B.C. 1263. Argonautic expedition. 1182. Æneas lands in Italy.

CHAPTER XIV.

THE age of theocracy was that time during which God was himself King and Ruler of His chosen people. It begins with the date at which He led them forth from their house of bondage in Egypt.

And God now saw fit to give special laws to His people, the following of which was to insure them God's blessing and protection. Moses was commanded to assemble all the tribes at the foot of Mount Sinai, which was covered with a thick darkness, out of which came thunderings and lightnings; and the voice of God spake to them, and said—

" I am the Lord thy God, who brought thee out of the land of Egypt, and out of the house of bondage.

    I. Thou shalt not have strange gods before me, &c.

    II. Thou shalt not take the name of the Lord thy God in vain.

    III. Remember that thou keep holy the Sabbath-day.

    IV. Honour thy father and thy mother.

    V. Thou shalt not kill.

    VI. Thou shalt not commit adultery.

    VII. Thou shalt not steal.

    VIII. Thou shalt not bear false witness against thy neighbour.

    IX. Thou shalt not covet thy neighbour's wife.

    X. Nor anything that is thy neighbour's."

These precepts,[1] with their developments,[2] were heard by all the people, who, seized with fear, said to Moses, " Speak thou to us, and we will hear; let not God speak to us, lest we die."

The Lord then said unto Moses, "Come up to me into the mount; and I will give thee tables of stone, and a law and commandments which I have written, that thou mayest teach them." And Moses was on Mount Sinai forty days and forty nights; and when God had made an end of communing with Moses, He gave unto him two tables of testimony—tables of stone—on which the decalogue[3] was written with the finger of God, which Moses brought down with him from the mountain.

But during the time Moses was on Mount Sinai, the people had offended God.

They thought Moses would not come back to them; and they remembered the idols[4] they had seen in Egypt, and obliged Aaron to make them a golden calf, unto which they offered sacrifice.

And God was very wroth with the people; but Moses interceded[5] with God for them, and after the most guilty had been punished, he obtained their pardon.

Moses began to carry out the commands which God had given him respecting the building of the tabernacle,[6] in which the ark of the covenant[7] was to be kept.

The tabernacle was divided into two compartments. The first of these contained the altar of incense,[8] the seven-branched candlestick, with lamps, and all the instruments used in the sacrifices.

The second, or inner chamber, was the holy of holies, containing the ark of the covenant—a box made of precious[9] wood, covered within and without with plates of pure gold, in which were preserved the tables of the law, or of the testimony,[10] Aaron's rod, and a measure of manna—that miraculous bread with which God fed His people during forty years in the desert. The lid of the ark was called the mercy-seat. It was made entirely of pure gold, and golden cherubim overshadowed it with their wings.

[1] Præ, before; capio, to take.
[2] De, from; volvo, I fold.
[3] Deka, ten; logos, a word, a treatise.
[4] From the Greek, eidolon, object.
[5] Inter, between; cedo, I go.
[6] Tabernaculum, Latin for tent—hence (Eng.) tavern.
[7] Con, together; venio, I come. Covenant, agreement.
[8] Incendo, to burn. From in, into; candeo, I become shining, I glow.

CHAPTER XV.

AARON was appointed[1] the high priest by Moses, and the whole of the tribe of Levi was attached[2] to the service of the tabernacle. The high priest was to instruct the people, as well as to consult[3] God on all emergencies.

After the many murmurings and revolts which had so often angered the Lord against the children of Israel, they added the crowning sin of despising[4] the Land of Promise to which they were being led.

They complained[5] of the difficulties and the dangers of invading Canaan; for though they knew it was a land flowing with milk and honey, yet the inhabitants, they said, were giants, and they feared them; and so the people murmured, and God said they should not go into Canaan; that they should wander forty years in the wilderness, and die in it, but that their children should possess[6] the land.

And God continued to feed His people, during the forty years they journeyed in the wilderness, with manna, which fell with the dew upon the camp in the night, and the people gathered it up and made cakes of it, and the taste was as the taste of fresh oil; and when the time of their probation was over, and they had entered Canaan, then the manna ceased falling.

Josue,[7] the successor of Moses, was appointed by God to lead His people into Canaan, and to disperse[8] the wicked inhabitants. When this was accomplished, the Land of Promise was divided amongst the twelve tribes of Israel, according to the number of the sons of Jacob. Thus was the promise of God unto Abraham fulfilled—"Unto thee and to thy seed will I give the land (of Canaan) for ever." The tribe of Levi alone had no land apportioned[9] to it, because it was devoted to the

[1] *Ad*, to; *pono*, I place. Syn.—put forward.
[2] *Ad*, to; *tango*, I touch. Syn.—belonging to.
[3] *Consulo*, I think over.   [4] *De*, down; *spicio*, I look.
[5] *Con*, together; *plango*, I weep, lament.
[6] *Possedio*, hold, settle in.
[7] Joshua, the same name as Jesus—God is my salvation; or, Whose help is Jehovah.—*Gesenius.*
[8] *Di*, apart: *spergo*. I scatter.   [9] *Ad*, to; *portio*, a part.

service of the tabernacle; "for the priesthood of the Lord was their inheritance."

The posterity of Joseph was divided into the two tribes of Ephraim and Manasses, according to the wish of Jacob.

After Josue, the Israelites were governed for more than 300 years by inspired[1] men, called judges, who defended the Israelites against the neighbouring tribes, nearly all of whom were enemies.

The judges are usually reckoned twelve, of whom Othoniel[2] (Otho-ni-el) was the first, and Samuel[3] the last, from B.C. 1405 to 1095.

Othoniel, the first judge, delivered the people from the servitude of Chusan, king of Mesopotamia.

Ehud, the second judge, released them from the power of Eglon, king of Moab; and Deborah, third judge, a prophetess, was the principal cause of their deliverance[4] out of the hands of Jabin, king of Canaan.

Gideon, fourth judge, subdued the Madianites.

Jephte, seventh judge, was the deliverer of the Israelites from the Ammonites. About this epoch, Troy was taken by the Greeks, B.C. 1184.

The Philistines (Phi-lis'-tines) were vanquished and driven back by Samson,[5] under the high priest Eli.

The high priest Eli was the eleventh judge; but he governed too feebly to repress[6] either the boldness of the enemies of Israel or the misconduct of his sons.

Samuel, twelfth judge, succeeded[7] Eli; and the Lord was with him, and he was established to be a prophet of the Lord. But when Samuel was old, he made his sons judges over Israel, and they walked not in his ways. Then the Israelites asked for a king to judge them, like all the nations.[8]

And the Lord said to Samuel, "Hearken unto their voice, and make them a king."

---

[1] *In*, into; *spiro*, I breathe.   [2] Lion of God.
[3] Samuel, Heard by God; or, The name of God.
[4] *De*, from; *libero*, I free.
[5] Samson, Sunlike; or, Like the sun.—*Gesenius.*
[6] *Re*, back; *premo*, I press.   [7] *Sub*, after; *cedo*, I go.
[8] *Natus*, born.

PERIOD V., OR TIME OF THE KINGDOM OF ALL ISRAEL, 120 YEARS. FROM B.C. 1095 TO 975.

SCRIPTURE HISTORY. B.C.	AFRICA.	ASIA.	EUROPE.
1095. Saul king of all Israel. 1055. David king of Juda, in Hebron. 1048. David king of all Israel. 1015. Solomon. 1012. Solomon begins the Temple. 1004. Temple dedicated. 975. End of the kingdom of all Israel.		1044. Ephesus, Miletus, and ten other Ionian colonies founded.	B.C. 1044. Greece founds the Ionian colonies.

CHAPTER XVI.

SAMUEL anointed Saul, of the tribe of Benjamin, first king of Israel. And Saul[1] reigned forty years; but, for his repeated disobedience to God's commands, his posterity was excluded from the throne.

David,[2] of the tribe of Juda, was next chosen by God, and anointed king by Samuel. Then began the fulfilment of Jacob's prophecy, who, in foretelling to each of his sons the destiny of his posterity, had said, "The sceptre[3] shall not depart from Juda until Shiloh[4] come." The Messiah[5] was born of the race of David.

After a glorious reign of forty years, David was succeeded by his son Solomon.[6] This young prince asked of God wisdom to judge his people, and he became the wisest, the greatest, and the most powerful king of any age; but, when he was old, he fell into sin, and his enemies rose up against him, and God announced to him that his kingdom would be divided.

---

[1] Saul, Asked.   [2] David, Beloved.   [3] Sceptre, means a Rod.
[4] Shiloh, of doubtful etymology—the most probable meaning is, The Desired One.
[5] Messiah, means the same as Christ, The Anointed; The Prince.
[6] Solomon, means the Pacific. This name is still used in Arabia as Solyman.

PERIOD VI, OR TIME OF THE TWO KINGDOMS, 254 YEARS.
FROM B.C. 975 TO 721.

SCRIPTURE HISTORY.		AFRICA.	ASIA.	EUROPE.
B.C. 975. Revolt of the Ten Tribes under Jeroboam.				
JUDA. 975. Roboam. 914. Elias and Eliseus. 838. Isaias, Osee, Joel, and Amos, prophets.	B.C. ISRAEL. 975. Jeroboam. 721. Destruction of Israel by Salmanasar, and dispersion of the Ten Tribes in Assyria.	B.C. 869. Carthage built by Dido.	B.C. 747. End of first Assyrian Empire.	B.C. 753. Rome founded by Romulus.

CHAPTER XVII

THEN it came to pass that Roboam, King David's grandson, refused the just demands of the people to diminish[1] the very heavy taxes imposed on them by Solomon.

Ten of the tribes of Israel separated themselves from Roboam and took Jeroboam as king. This made a complete split in the kingdom. The tribes of Juda and of Benjamin formed the kingdom of Juda, of which Jerusalem continued to be the capital[2] or chief city; whilst Samaria[3] formed the kingdom of Israel.

It was at Jerusalem that the temple of Solomon was built in honour of God. Its magnificence[4] placed it amongst the wonders of the world. It was consecrated[5] B.C. 1004.

The kings of Israel withdrew themselves and their subjects from worshipping in the temple, and from serving God, as they feared the people might return to their allegiance[6] to the kings

---

[1] *De* or *Di*, from; *minuo*, I lessen.
[2] Capital, from *caput*, head.
[3] Samaria, the most central of the four provinces into which the Romans divided Palestine. Its chief city was Samaria, the capital of the kingdom of Israel. The Samaritans had their chief temple on Mount Garizim.
[4] *Magnum*, great; *facio*, I make.   [5] *Con*, together; *secro*, I make holy.
[6] *Ad*, to; *ligo*, to bind. Old French word.

of the house of David.   Thus idolatry[1] was established in
Samaria.

But even in the midst of all these wars and offences God
did not forsake His people.   He sent them prophets from time
to time, who announced to them coming events, and who
proved, by miracles, their mission[2] to be real.

Thus mercifully did God act towards them, that they might
not forget Him or His commandments.

Elias[3] the prophet was first sent to reprove the impiety[4] of
Achab, king of Israel, and to destroy the worship of Baal;[5] and
he was taken up into heaven in a chariot of fire.

His disciple, Eliseus,[6] delivered Samaria from the Syrians.[7]
These two prophets have left us no written instructions.

There are, however, a good number of books by the other
prophets.   The four principal of these, called the Great Prophets, have predicted the most important events relating to the
fall of Jerusalem and the coming of the Messiah.

Isaias[8] writes so vividly[9] of these events, and, above all, of
Christ, (the God-Man,) that he appears rather an historian than
a prophetical writer.   He began to prophesy in the year B.C. 776,
at which period the Greeks date their first Olympiad.[10]

Jeremias[11] laments the crimes of Jerusalem, and weeps over
its ruins.   These lamentations are very beautiful; and Baruch,
his secretary, has written some admirable things upon the
Babylonish captivity.

Ezechiel[12] (E-ze'ch-i-el) and his revelations carry us into the
very presence of the Deity.   All that is mysterious would seem
to have been revealed to him.

[1] From a compound Greek word, meaning serving of images.
[2] Sending, from *mitto*, I send.
[3] Elias, My God is Jehovah.
[4] *In*, not; *pietas*, piety.
[5] *Bel* meant, The Sun, also Lord, in Chaldee.
[6] Eliseus, To whom God is salvation.—*Gesenius.*
[7] Syria, called in Scripture Aram, extended along the Mediterranean,
from Asia Minor to Egypt.   It embraced Phœnicia and Palestine.   It contained the two mountain-chains, called Lebanon and Anti-Libanus.   Its chief
river was the Orontes; and its principal cities were Laodicea, Antioch, Pal-
myra, and Damascus.
[8] Isaias, The Salvation of Jehovah.   [9] *Vivus*, alive. Vividly, life-like.
[10] Olympiad, so called from the national games of the Greeks, which occurred
every four years.
[11] Jeremias, Whom God appointed.
[12] Ezechiel, Whom God strengthens.

Daniel,[1] a sublime[2] prophet and an able minister, predicted the exact epoch[3] at which the Messiah would come, and proclaimed,[4] in the midst of idolaters, the only true God. He was cast into a den of lions; but God sent His angel to shut the lions' mouths, and Daniel was taken out unhurt; and Darius, king of the Medes and Persians, made a decree, that in every dominion of his kingdom, men should tremble and fear before the God of Daniel, "for He is the living God."

CHAPTER XVIII.

THE twelve Lesser Prophets had each his mission. Osee recounts[5] and denounces the crimes of the children of Israel, above all, those of their priests and princes.

Joel predicts the ruin of Jerusalem and the coming of the Holy Ghost.

Amos foretells and bewails the desolation of Juda, and of the neighbouring people; the ruin of the temple, and its restoration.

Abdias announces the coming of Christ and of His Church (the reign of the Saviour).

Jona, who had consoled[6] Juda and prophesied a defeat[7] of the Syrians, is sent to preach repentance at Nineve (Nin'-e-ve).

Micheas named Bethlehem[8] as the place of Christ's nativity. At this time Rome, destined to be the centre of the Christian religion, was founded in the West, B.C. 753.

Nahum prophesies the ruin of Nineve and the desolation of Alexandria and Egypt.

Habacuc (Hab'-a-cuc) is astonished at the prosperity[9] of the wicked. He is shewn by God that the just must live by faith, and that the prosperity of the wicked is not to be trusted.

Sophonias exhorts[10] Israel to repent, and predicts[11] its conversion.

---

[1] Daniel, The Judge of God.
[2] Sublime, very high, lofty.
[3] Epoch, division of time. A Greek word, meaning a pause or stop.
[4] Pro, before; clamo, I call.
[5] French, raconter, to tell.
[6] Con, together; solor, I comfort.
[7] De, from; factus, done. Undone, worsted.
[8] Bethlehem, The House of Bread.
[9] Pro, before; spero, I hope. Thriving.
[10] Ex, out of; hortor, to urge.
[11] Præ, before; dico, I say.

Aggeus (Agg'eus) is witness of the rebuilding of the temple, and promises greater glory to the second temple than was given to the first.

Zacharias foresees the priesthood of Christ and the mission[1] of the apostles,[1] the overthrow of idolatry and the triumph[2] of the Church. The Messiah was to come as the Prince of Peace, and was to be sold for thirty pieces of silver.

Malachias[3] speaks of a new sacrifice, and of a pure oblation,[4] which was to follow the abrogation[5] of the old law.

It was thus that God kept alive the true worship amongst the children of Jacob, and the belief in the coming of the Messiah. But He severely punished their infidelities.[6]

PERIOD VII., OR TIME OF THE KINGDOM OF JUDA AND OF THE CAPTIVITY, 185 YEARS. FROM B.C. 721 TO 536.

SCRIPTURE HISTORY.	AFRICA.	ASIA.	EUROPE.
B.C. 710. Sennacherib's army destroyed. 606. Captivity of Juda begins. 587. Jerusalem destroyed by Nabuchadonosor. 536. Return from Captivity.		B.C. 538. Babylon taken. 536. Cyrus sole monarch of the Medo-Persian empire.	

CHAPTER XIX.

THIS period commences with the destruction of the ten tribes, and their being carried captive into Assyria, and there dispersed among the heathen. It ends with the return of the two tribes of the race of David from captivity, B.C. 536.

The kingdom of Israel had been destroyed under the seventeenth king, Osee, by Salmanasar, (Sal-ma-na'-sar,) who led

---

[1] Apostles, from a Greek word, The sent.
[2] Means a victory, or victorious march.
[3] Malachi, Messenger of Jehovah.
[4] Ob, before; fero, I carry. Offering is the same as oblation.
[5] Ab, away; rogo, I ask. To do away.
[6] In, not; fidelis, faithful.

the ten tribes captive, and dispersed them throughout Assyria.[1] This was towards the year B.C. 721.

Ezechias then reigned in Juda. He served God, and was delivered from the invasion of Sennacherib, the son and successor of Salmanasar. The army of this mighty king was smitten by an angel of the Lord, and totally annihilated,[2] and he himself was assassinated by two of his sons.

But, a century after, the kings of Juda also deserved punishment, and Nabuchadonosor, (Nab-u-chad-on'-o-sor,) king of Babylon and Nineve, took Jerusalem, destroyed the temple, and carried away all the people. Then began the captivity of Babylon, or of the two tribes of the race of David, B.C. 606. The king, Jechonias,[3] or Joachin, was also led captive. And it came to pass, in the seven-and-thirtieth year of his captivity, that Evil-merodach, son of Nabuchadonosor, took Joachin of Juda out of prison, and treated him as a king. Thus " the sceptre did not depart from Juda."

Towards the time of the captivity, the Holy Scriptures relate many wonderful events which testify to the power of the Almighty, as well as to His love for His chosen people.

Whilst Israel was in captivity, and dispersed throughout the kingdom of Assyria, Holofernes (Hol-o-fer'-nes) was sent into Judea to complete its conquest. He besieged Bethulia,[4] (Beth-u'-li-a,) and reduced it to the last extremity,[5] when a virtuous widow, named Judith,[6] determined to devote[7] herself to save her country. She went over to the camp of the Assyrians, and cut off the head of Holofernes whilst he slept, and carried it back with her to Bethulia. His army was then easily put to flight and dispersed.

Tobias was one of the Israelitish captives, and he served God

---

[1] Assyria, one of the most ancient empires in the world. It was at first confined to a district north-east of Mesopotamia, stretching along the east bank of the Tigris. It was afterwards greatly enlarged by conquest, embracing Babylonia, Mesopotamia, Armenia, &c., and reaching to the Persian Gulf. Its chief city was Nineve, on the Tigris, founded, according to tradition, by Ninus.

[2] *Ad*, to; *nihil*, nothing. Means reduced to nothing, or destroyed.

[3] Jechonias, Whom God appointed.

[4] Bethulia perhaps means Virgin City. It appears to have commanded one of the passes to Jerusalem.

[5] *Ex*, out of; *exterus*, outside, last. Extremity, end.

[6] Judith means, when used adverbially, Jewishly.—*Gesenius.*

[7] *De*, from; *voveo*, I vow.

in Nineve as he had done in Samaria. God had afflicted him with blindness; but the angel Raphael,[1] (Ra'-pha-el,) under the appearance of a young Israelite, had conducted the son of Tobias on a journey, and on his return Tobias recovered his sight, by applying a remedy[2] given to his son by the angel. The spirit of prophecy fell upon the elder Tobias after the angel had left him and his family; and he foretold the glory of Jerusalem, and that the time would come when the Gentiles would worship the Lord God of Israel.

During the seventy years of the captivity in Babylon, the proud spirit of the rebellious house of Juda was broken; and the thoughts of the people were brought back to the God of their fathers, and they lamented their disobedience and past forgetfulness of God's favours.

And God gave them prophets, as He had done before, to be guides and comforters to His people during this period of probation.

CHAPTER XX.

DANIEL, one of the children of the captivity of the two tribes of Juda, B.C. 605, was taken at an early age, with three other young Hebrews, Ananias, (An-a-ni'-as,) Misael, (Mis'-a-el,) and Azarias, (Az-a-ri'-as,) and brought up at the court of Nabuchadonosor.

Daniel interpreted a dream for the king, and was made ruler over the whole province of Babylon; and he gave to his three friends, Ananias, Misael, and Azarias, posts of honour under him, and their names were changed to Sidrach, Misach, and Abdenego, (Ab-de'-ne-go.)

Now the king having set up a statue of gold to be worshipped on the plain of Dura, in the province of Babylon, Sidrach, Misach, and Abdenego, would not worship the golden image, and they were thrown, by order of Nabuchadonosor, into a burning fiery furnace. But an angel came to them in the furnace, and the fire touched them not at all, nor did them any harm.

Now Nabuchadonosor was not sufficiently[3] admonished;[4] his

[1] Raphael, Whom God healed.
[2] Sufficit, it is enough.
[3] Re, again; medeor, I mend, or heal.
[4] Ad, to; moneo, I advise.

pride was displeasing to God, who afflicted him with madness, and he fled from men, and did eat grass as oxen. He continued in this state for seven years. Then he understood the power of the Most High, and he glorified the God of heaven, and ordered his people to do likewise.

Another king, Darius Artaxerxes, son of Hystaspes, (Hy-sta's-pes,) called in Scripture, Assuerus, (As-su-e'-rus,) had married a young Israelitish woman named Esther,[1] whom her uncle, Mardocheus, (Mar-do-che'-us,) had brought up, and still aided by his advice. Aman, a favourite of the king, having remarked that Mardocheus did not bow to him, or shew him the reverence [2] he received from others, determined to revenge himself, and to bring about a general massacre [3] of the Jews throughout the kingdom. Esther was told of this by Mardocheus; and, after having prayed and humbled [4] herself before God, she sought Assuerus, and made suit for her own life and that of her people. Assuerus granted all her requests,[5] and Aman was hanged on the gibbet which he had prepared for Mardocheus the Jew. About this time the empire of the Assyrians passed into the hands of the Medes and Persians.[6]

Baltassar, (Bal-tas'-sar,) the last king of Babylon, was guilty of many crimes, and added to them that of the profanation[7] of sacred things. He made a great feast to a thousand of his lords; and he had the golden and silver vessels brought, which Nabuchadonosor had taken out of the temple at Jerusalem, and the king and his guests drank in them.

In the same hour a hand appeared writing on the wall of the palace, and none of the wise men could read the writing.

[1] Esther was her Persian name, meaning fortune, star, happiness. Her Hebrew name was Hadassa.—*Gesenius.*

[2] *Re*, again; *vereor*, I fear.   [3] Massacre (Fr.) means slaughter.

[4] *Humilis*, from *humus*, the ground. Syn.—lowered.

[5] *Re*, back; *quæro*, I seek. Demands.

[6] Media was situated between the Caspian Sea, Armenia, Assyria, and Persia. It was divided into Great Media and Media-Atropatene. Ecbatana was its capital. It was at length subdued by Persia. Persia was an ancient empire, containing Assyria, Armenia, Media, Syria, and Asia. At the height of its power it contained twelve provinces.

Persia proper, the original province from which the Persians issued to invade the neighbouring countries, was situated south of Media, near the Persian Gulf. Its capital was Persepolis, burnt by Alexander the Great, king of Macedon, who conquered the Persian empire, and divided it among his generals, about B.C. 323.

[7] *Pro*, before (not allowed to enter); *fanum*, the sanctuary.

Daniel was now called, and he read what was written, and this is the interpretation :—"God hath numbered thy kingdom and finished it. Thou art weighed in the balance[1] and found wanting. Thy kingdom is divided, and given to the Medes and Persians."

The Median and Persian army, under Cyrus, had for two years besieged[2] Babylon, and that very night, while the king and the inhabitants were revelling, the great work of turning off the waters of the river Euphrates, which ran through Babylon, was finished, and the besieging army marched through the dry bed of the river, and the city was taken. Baltassar was surprised at his banquet, and slain, and Darius[3] the Median took the kingdom.

This terminated the seventieth year of the Jewish captivity, from the fall of Jerusalem, and the carrying away of Jechonias into Babylon, fulfilling the period predicted by Jeremias, who said, that "the desolation of Juda and the triumph of Babylon should last seventy years." Moreover, Isaias, 200 years before, had named Cyrus as the deliverer of Israel. And Cyrus, having conquered Babylon, permitted the captives to return into their country, giving them back the sacred vessels which Baltassar had profaned.

[1] *Bis*, double; *lanx*, a dish.
[2] *Be*, by; *siége* (Fr.), a sitting down.
[3] Darius (Hystaspes) reigned B.C. 521.

PERIOD VIII. BEGINS WITH THE RETURN FROM CAPTIVITY, AND ENDS WITH THE BIRTH OF JESUS CHRIST. FROM B.C. 536 TO A.D. 1, VULGAR ERA.

SCRIPTURE HISTORY.	ASIA.	AFRICA.	EUROPE.
B.C.			
536. Captivity ends.			
515. Dedication of the second Temple.			
430. Bible history ends.			
332. Alexander enters the Temple.		B.C. 285. Septuagint translation.	
170. Antiochus Epiphanes takes Jerusalem.			272. Romans possess all Italy.
163. Judas Maccabæus.			
135. Apocrypha ends.	B C.		
63. Jerusalem taken by Pompey.	65. Syria made a Roman province.		
40. Herod made king of Judea.			
37. Death of Antigonus, last of the Maccabees or Asmonean family.		30. Egypt a Roman province.	27. Octavius called Augustus. Rome an empire.
A.D.			
1. Birth of Christ.			

CHAPTER XXI.

JERUSALEM was not rebuilt, because the neighbouring people feared to see it rise again into power. But Nehemias obtained of Artaxerxes[1] permission to build its walls, and thus to protect the temple (which had been rebuilt by Zorobabel and Esdras, B.C. 515,) as well as the dwellings of the Jews.

This name of Jew[2] was at length given to the Hebrews because the tribe of Juda formed the principal part of those who returned, whilst the ten tribes remained and were dispersed in Asia and Egypt. The name of Juda was also retained. The rebuilding of the walls by Nehemias occurred the year B.C. 445, and Daniel had announced that, counting from that time, the Messias would accomplish His work after seventy weeks of years. It is easy to reckon and to ascertain that the prophecy was verified.[3]

[1] There were three kings of Persia of this name. The Artaxerxes here alluded to was surnamed Longimanus, long-handed. B.C. 464.

[2] Jew, or rather Juda; the name means famous, celebrated.—*Gesenius.*

[3] *Verum,* true; *fio,* I make.

The Jewish republic[1] remained unmolested[2] for some years, under the protection[3] of the kings of Persia.   Alexander the Great, the conqueror of Darius, passing by Jerusalem, visited the high priest, and made rich offerings to the temple.   Alexander died at the age of thirty-three, and his generals divided his vast empire into four separate kingdoms—Greece, Asia Minor, Syria, and Egypt.   Seleucus Nicanor made himself king of Syria, and permitted the Jews to live according to their laws, and to be governed by their high priests.

After the death of Seleucus, Palestine fell under the rule of Egypt.   Ptolemy Philadelphius[4] wished a Greek translation[5] of the sacred writings of the Hebrews.   This translation is called the Septuagint[6] version.[7]

The Jews were at first favoured by Seleucus Philopator, (Phil-o'-pa-tor,) who, after Antiochus (Ant-ti'-o-chus) the Great, and Ptolemy Epiphanes, united Palestine to his own dominions;[8] but false reports were brought to him respecting the treasures hidden in the temple.   He sent Heliodorus to force an entrance into it, notwithstanding the opposition of the high priest Onias, but scarcely had he done so, when he was thrown down and struck by two angels armed with rods : his life was spared at the prayer of Onias.

The Jews were now much corrupted by their intercourse with the refined[9] but immoral Greeks; and Antiochus Epiphanes, the king of Syria, thought that by undermining and destroying their religion, he should consolidate[10] his empire—he found, however, more resistance than he anticipated.[11]

Eleazar, one of the chief of the scribes, refused to submit to the edicts[12] of this prince, and was cruelly put to death because he would not eat of things forbidden by the law of Moses. Seven brothers and their mother were likewise most cruelly tortured and put to death by the tyrant, because they would not break the law of the only true God.

[1] *Res publica*, common wealth.   [2] *Un*, not; *molior*, I move, attack, or destroy.
[3] *Pro*, before ; *tectus*, a roof, a covering.
[4] Philadelphius, loving his brother—so called ironically because he killed one of his brothers. king of Egypt—died 246 B.C.
[5] *Trans*, over ; *latus*, carried.
[6] Seventy.   From the seventy doctors (or seventy-two).
[7] *Versio*, turning, or change.   [8] *Dominus*, lord, lordship.
[9] Refined, polished.   [10] *Con*, together ; *solidus*, solid.   Strengthened.
[11] *Ante*, before ; *capio*, I take.   [12] *E*, out of ; *dico*. I say.   Decisions. laws.

CHAPTER XXII.

MATTATHIAS, (Mat-ta-thi'-as,) a priest, with his five sons, of whom the third, named Judas Maccabæus, (Mac-ca-bæ'-us,) was remarkable for his courage,[1] protested[2] against the impious commands of the king. They left the city, and gathered around them an army of men zealous as themselves for the law. From the mountains, amongst which they had taken refuge,[3] they made inroads into the city of Jerusalem, overthrew the Gentile[4] altars, and succeeded at length in rousing the Jews against the tyrant who refused them the liberty to follow their religion, which had been previously[5] allowed them by treaty.

On the death of Mattathias, his son, Judas Maccabæus, put to flight all the generals sent against him by Antiochus. He entered Jerusalem, recovered the temple, and restored the daily sacrifice. Antiochus died miserably,[6] devoured by worms, B.C. 164. The contentions[7] amongst the Jews induced Judas Maccabæus to seek an alliance[8] with the Roman people; he sent ambassadors[9] to Rome, who brought back from the Romans a friendly letter to the Jews, accepting them as allies. Thus began the first intercourse with Rome, which ended in the crucifixion of the Messias, by the sentence[10] of the Roman governor of Palestine, and in the total destruction of their holy city and nation.

Judas was slain in battle against Nicanor, (Ni-ca'-nor,) a general of the usurper Demetrius, king of Syria. His brothers, Jonathan and Simon, succeeded Judas, and the sovereignty[11] of Judea remained in the family of the Maccabees (Mac'-ca-bees) for a hundred years.

The dissensions[12] between the Jews became more and more

---

[1] Courage (Fr.), bravery. Lat. *cor*, the heart.
[2] Protested, bore witness.
[3] *Re*, back; *fugio*, I fly. A shelter.
[4] *Gens*, a people (that is, not the Jews).
[5] *Præ*, before; *via*, the way. Before.
[6] *Miser*, wretched.
[7] *Con*, together; *tendo*, I stretch.
[8] Bond of friendship. *Ad*, to; *ligo*, I tie.
[9] Ambassadors—Spanish, *embaxador*—messengers.
[10] Sentence, judgment. [11] Rule.
[12] *Dis*, asunder; *sentio*, I feel. Quarrel.

sanguinary,[1] and the Romans at length interfered.[2] Pompey, the Roman general, besieged Jerusalem, B.C. 63. But the people continued to be governed by one of themselves; they found, however, that their freedom was very limited.

Twenty years after this date, Herod the Idumean (Id-u-mæ'-an) was recognised as king of Judea by the Roman emperor Augustus, by Anthony, and the senate. Herod not being of Jewish blood, the sceptre passed away from Juda, and the people became a tributary[3] kingdom of the Roman empire. But the time now drew nigh for the coming of the Messias. In the Idumean Herod was fulfilled another prophecy of Isaac's, who, to console Esau, after Jacob had secured[4] the chief of the paternal[5] blessings, had told him that one day he would throw off the yoke. Esau, named Edom, was father of the Idumeans, and thus became head or master of the house of Jacob or Israel.

At this period[6] the writings of the Old Testament cease, B.C. 430. The Old Testament is a collection[7] of books written by inspired authors before the coming of Christ. It is not a connected[8] work, as some people seem to imagine,[9] who speak of reading the Bible as if it contained instruction adapted for all intelligences.[10] The books of which it consists[11] were given at different periods, and in proportion to the wants and the comprehension,[12] the manners and customs of mankind. The Bible[13] includes also the New Testament, or the New Law, given by Jesus Christ, the true Messias, who came not to destroy, but to fulfil or perfect the law of Moses. These books were written by the apostles of Christ during the first century of the Christian era.[14] They begin with the books of the four evangelists,[15] which contain the life and the miracles of Jesus Christ himself.

[1] Bloody.
[2] *Inter*, between; *fero*, I carry.
[3] Subject people paying taxes to a foreign state.
[4] Secured, made safe.
[5] Fatherly, from *pater*, father.
[6] Time.
[7] *Co*, together; *ligo*, I bind.
[8] *Con*, together; *necto*, I weave.
[9] Image, picture.
[10] Minds.
[11] *Con*, together; *sto*, stand. It is made up of.
[12] *Con*, together; *prehendo*, I grasp.
[13] Bible, from the Greek, *biblon*, book.
[14] Era, a division of time. Thus the Christian era includes the 1860 years since the Incarnation.
[15] *Evangelistes*, a bringer of good news. *God*, good; *spell* (Old Eng.), story.

PERIOD IX. FROM THE BIRTH OF JESUS CHRIST—A.M. 4004 TO A.D. 101—TO THE DEATH OF THE LAST OF THE APOSTLES.

APOSTOLIC AGE.

A.D.	ASIA.	A.D.	EUROPE.
1.	Birth of Jesus Christ.		
30.	Jesus Christ is baptized by St John, and begins His ministry.		
33.	Crucifixion.		Nero burns Rome and accuses the
34.	Conversion of St Paul.		Christians of the act.
51.	First Council held by the apostles at Jerusalem.	64.	It gives rise to the First Persecution.
		66.	St Peter and St Paul both martyred
70.	Titus destroys Jerusalem.		on the same day, June 29, at Rome.
101.	St John dies at Ephesus.	95.	Second Persecution under Domitian.

CHAPTER XXIII.

IN the days of Herod,[1] the king of Juda, there was a certain priest named Zacharias, of the tribe of Levi, and his wife Elizabeth,[2] of the tribe of Juda, and they were both just before God.

And they had no child, and now were both well stricken in years.

And it came to pass, as Zacharias was offering incense in the temple, the angel Gabriel[3] came unto him, and said, "Thy wife Elizabeth shall bear thee a son, and thou shalt call his name John,[4] and he shall be filled with the Holy Ghost."

This John was he of whom it was written in the prophets, "Behold, I send my angel before thy face, who shall prepare thy way before thee. The voice of one crying in the wilderness, 'Prepare ye the way of the Lord, make his paths straight.'"

Mary,[5] the cousin of Elizabeth, and daughter of Joi'-a-kim[6] and of Anna,[7] had been consecrated to God from her infancy,[8]

---

[1] Herod the Great, son of Antipater, was made king of Judea by the Romans B.C. 38. After a wicked reign of 37 years he died a wretched death.

[2] Elizabeth, To whom God is an oath. Who swears by God; that is, a worshipper of God.

[3] Gabriel, The Man of God.

[4] John, Whom God gave.

[5] *Mara* means bitter, to shew the bitter dolours or sorrows of our Lady.

[6] Or Joachim, Whom God appointed.

[7] Anna, Gracious.

[8] *In not : faus speaking*

and had dwelt in the temple until she was fifteen. Her mother, Saint Anna, had brought her up in the fear of the Lord; and the blessed Virgin being exempt [1] from all sin, was perfect in all her ways.

And in the sixth month of the same year that the angel Gabriel had announced to Zacharias the birth of John the Baptist, the same angel was sent by God to a little city in Galilee,[2] called Nazareth,[3] where the blessed Virgin then dwelt. And the angel being come in, said unto her, "Hail, full of grace, the Lord is with thee: blessed art thou among women."

Mary was troubled at these words, and knew not what to think. Then the angel said, "Fear not, Mary, for thou hast found grace with God. Behold, thou shalt bring forth a son, and thou shalt call his name Jesus.[4] He shall be great, and shall be called the Son of the most High; and the Lord God shall give unto him the throne of David his father: and he shall live in the house of Jacob for ever, and of his kingdom there shall be no end."

Then Mary said to the angel, "How shall this be?"

And the angel answering, said to her, "The Holy Ghost shall come upon thee, and the power of the most High shall overshadow thee; and, therefore, the Holy which shall be born of thee, shall be called the Son of God."

And Mary said, "Behold the handmaid of the Lord; be it done to me according to thy word." And the angel departed from her.

Soon after the annunciation, Mary went into the hill country, into a city of Juda, to visit her cousin St Elizabeth.

And she entered into the house of Zacharias, and saluted [5] Elizabeth.

And it came to pass that, when St Elizabeth heard the

---

[1] *Ex*, out of; *emptus*, bought.

[2] Galilee, the most northern of the four provinces into which the Romans divided the Holy Land. In it were situated Lake Gennesareth or Tiberias, and Mount Tabor. Its principal city at that time was Capharnaum or Tiberias, on the lake of that name.

[3] Nazareth, meaning "The Flower," lies hid in a lovely basin. It is now a very small town, and has subsided (or been built) down hill, more into the valley. The inhabitants are mostly Christians, and of these 1000 are Catholics. —*Patterson*, p. 273.

[4] God is my Salvation.

[5] From *salus*, health. Hail

salutation of Mary, she was filled with the Holy Ghost, and cried, " Whence is this to me, that the mother of my Lord should come to me? For, lo, as soon as the voice of thy salutation sounded in my ears, the babe leaped in my womb for joy."

And at that moment, when the child had leaped for joy, he was purified [1] from all original sin ; and when St John came into the world, three months after, he was born in a state of grace.

During these three months the blessed Virgin abode with St Elizabeth, and then returned to her own house.

CHAPTER XXIV.

AND it came to pass, that soon after Mary's return to Nazareth, there went forth a decree from Augustus [2] Cesar, the Roman emperor, [3] that all the inhabitants of his empire and its dependent [4] states were to be enrolled, each person in his own city.

Now St Joseph, a good and a holy man, of the house and lineage of David, had been chosen of God to act as protector [5] and adopted father to the Divine child and His mother, and is called in Scripture the husband of the blessed Virgin.

And Joseph went up from Galilee, out of the city of Nazareth, to Beth-le-hem, in Judea, with Mary, to be enrolled there.

And so it was, that, while they were there, the days were accomplished for Mary to be delivered. And she brought forth her first-born, the incarnate [6] Son of God, and wrapped Him in swaddling clothes, and laid Him in a manger ; because there was no room for them in the inn.

At the time of the nativity [7] of our blessed Lord in a cave, which was used as a stable, there were some shepherds in the neighbourhood of the town, keeping watch over their flock by night.

[1] *Pur,* from a word meaning fire; *fio,* I make. To purify, is to clear or clean.

[2] Augustus Cesar reigned from B.C. 31 to A.D. 14.

[3] Commander-in-chief, the name of the sovereigns of Rome after Augustus.

[4] *De,* from; *pendeo,* I hang.

[5] *Pro,* before; *tego,* I cover.

[6] *In,* into; *caro,* the flesh.　　　　[7] Birth.

And an angel announced to them that Christ, the promised Messias,[1] was born—an event for which all Judea had been waiting, and the fulfilment of which the prophets had predicted would occur about this time. The shepherds, therefore, were not surprised at the announcement of the angel : "Behold, I bring you good tidings of great joy, which shall be to all the people. For unto you is born this day, in the city of David, a Saviour, who is Christ the Lord."   •

And suddenly there was with the angel a multitude [2] of the heavenly host, praising God, and saying,

"Glory to God in the highest, and on earth peace towards men of good will."

The shepherds then hastened to Bethlehem, and found Mary and Joseph, and the Babe lying in a manger, as the angel had told them ; and when they had seen Him, they returned from thence, praising God ; and they made known the saying which had been told them concerning this Child.

The prophecy of Balaam, that "there shall come a star out of Jacob, and a sceptre shall rise out of Israel," which the Spirit of God had put into his mouth long ages before, in the time of Moses, and which had been spread abroad among the people in the far East, had been remembered, and had made a deep impression.[3]

Now when Jesus was born, there came wise men from the East, who had noticed [4] the rise of a new star, or a meteor,[5] in the heavens. These strangers, knowing the prophecy, had journeyed all the way to Jerusalem, to seek and to worship this King of the Jews, whose star they had seen in the east, and whose birth was to happen at that time, as had been so long foretold.

When Herod, the king, heard these things, he was troubled, and he consulted the chief priests and scribes,[6] and found that Christ was to be born in Bethlehem of Judea ; and Herod also inquired of the three wise men from the East at what time the star appeared.

Herod sent them to Bethlehem to search for the child, and he said, "When ye have found him, bring me word, and I will come and worship him also."

And the wise men departed; and, lo, the star which they had seen in the east went before them, till it came and stood over where the Child was.

And when they were come into the house, they saw the child with Mary His mother, and they fell down and adored Him; and presented unto Him gifts—gold, frankincense, and myrrh.[1]   And being warned by God in a dream, they returned not to Herod, but departed into their own country another way.

CHAPTER XXV.

FORTY days after the birth of Christ, Mary and Joseph brought Him to Jerusalem, to present Him to the Lord in the temple, according to the law of Moses.

And it had been revealed by the Holy Ghost to a just and devout[2] man, named Simeon, who lived in Jerusalem, that he should not see death before he had seen the Christ of the Lord.

And he came by the Spirit into the temple, and when the parents[3] brought in the child Jesus, Simeon took Him in his arms, and blessed Him, and said, "Lord, now lettest thou thy servant depart in peace, for mine eyes have seen thy salvation."

And Anna, a prophetess, coming in that instant, gave thanks likewise unto the Lord, and spoke of Him to all those who had looked for redemption in Jerusalem.

Now Herod, the king of Juda, feared that he should have a rival[4] in this long-looked for King of the Jews, of whose spiritual mission he had no conception.   When, therefore, he asked the three magi, or wise men of the East, to bring him word where they had found the child, that Herod might also go and worship Him, his real intention was to have Him put to death.

Then Herod, when he saw that the wise men did not return,

[1] The two last are the productions of plants still growing in Arabia, and are now used for incense in Catholic Churches, and for other purposes.
[2] Devout, devoted. Vowed to God.
[3] *Pario*, I bring forth.
[4] Rival, from *rivus*, bank. It means properly, a proprietor of the opposite bank of a river to your own. Hence, an opponent.

was exceeding[1] wroth, and sent forth and slew all the children that were in Bethlehem and in the neighbouring country, from two years old and under, according to the time which he had diligently[2] inquired of the wise men.

This cruel act, however, was of no avail,[3] for God warned Joseph in a dream, saying, "Arise, take the child and His mother, and flee into Egypt." And they remained there in safety until the death of Herod, which happened the same year.

When Herod was dead, Joseph was again instructed in a dream to return into the land of Israel with the child and His mother. And they returned to Nazareth, and dwelt there, that it might be fulfilled which was spoken by the prophets, "He shall be called a Naz-a-rene."

Tradition tells us that Joseph carried on the trade of a carpenter,[4] and that the Son of God assisted His adopted father in this humble occupation ;[5] whilst his holy mother, though of the royal[6] lineage[7] of David, thought it not beneath her to attend to the duties of her house.

It is said in Scripture that Jesus was subject to His parents, and that He grew in wisdom and age and grace with God and men ; and thus the perfections of His Divine nature were more and more developed and made manifest.

At the age of twelve years He went up to Jerusalem with Mary and Joseph, to the feast of the passover ; for from that age upwards every Jew had to attend[8] three times in the year, at each great solemnity of religion.

And as they returned, Jesus tarried behind in Jerusalem ; and His parents went a day's journey before they found that He was not with them, and they turned back again to seek Him.

At the end of three days they found Him in the temple, sitting in the midst of the doctors, both hearing them and asking questions ; and all that heard Him were astonished at His understanding and answers.

[1] *Ex*, out of ; *cedo*, I go. Exceeding, out of the way.
[2] *Diligo*, I love or choose out ; from *di* and *lego*, I choose. Diligently, fondly, carefully.
[3] Avail, use, or good. *Valeo*, I am of value.
[4] From *carpentum*, late Latin, a chariot. Any artificer who works in wood.
[5] *Ob*, against ; *capio*, I take. Occupied, taken up.
[6] From the French, *roi*, king. Royal, kingly.
[7] Lineage, family, or descent.   [8] *Ad*, to ; *tendo*, I stretch.

And His mother gently reproved Him for leaving them, to which he replied, "Know ye not that I must be about my Father's business?"

He then went down with them to Nazareth; and His mother kept all these sayings in her heart.

CHAPTER XXVI.

DURING thirty years of His life, Mary had her son near her. Then the time had arrived for Him to go forth and to begin His public ministry.[1]

John Baptist,[2] the forerunner of our Lord, had already left the desert, in which he had dwelt from his childhood, to preach and to baptize.

And he came into the country about Judea, exhorting[3] the people to repent, baptizing all those who repented, and who came to him confessing[4] their sins.

And John said to them, "I indeed baptize you with water; but one mightier than I cometh, He shall baptize with the Holy Ghost and with fire."

And one day John saw Jesus coming unto him, and he cried, "Behold the Lamb of God, behold Him who taketh away the sin of the world."

And Jesus was baptized by John in the Jordan, and straightway coming up out of the water, he saw the heavens opened, and the Spirit, like a dove, descending upon Him.

And there came a voice from heaven, saying, "Thou art my beloved Son, in whom I am well pleased."

From that time His disciples[5] began to gather round Him. The first was Andrew, and soon after his brother Simon, to whom Jesus said, "Thou art Simon, the son of Jona, and thou shalt be called Cephas,[6] or Peter, that is, a stone." And at a later period Jesus further explained His reason for giving this name to him, and said, "Thou art Peter, and upon this Peter,

[1] Ministry, service.
[2] Baptist. *Bapto*, I dip (Greek).
[3] *Ex*, out of; *hortor*, I urge, excite.
[4] *Con*, together; *fiteor*, I say.
[5] From *disco*, I learn.
[6] *Cepha* is the Syriac, *Petros* the Greek, for stone.

or rock, I will build my church, and the gates of hell shall not prevail against it."

The number of Christ's disciples began to increase. From amongst them He chose twelve to preach His doctrine[1] unto all nations, and these consequently were called apostles.[2]

And Christ drew after Him great multitudes, wherever He went, attracted[3] by the authority and the charm with which He spoke, as well as astonished at His miracles, and at the wonderful way in which He healed all manner of sickness and of disease among the people.

And Jesus and His disciples were at a marriage in Cana of Galilee. And when the people at the marriage wanted wine, Jesus bade them fill six waterpots which were there with water, and then He told them to draw forth, and the water was found to be changed into wine; and this was the first miracle which Christ did.

Now, Jesus having heard that Herod the tetrarch,[4] the son of king Herod, who had sought the life of Jesus in His infancy, had shut up John in prison, withdrew into Galilee, passing through Samaria, and being wearied with his journey, sat down to rest on the well called Jacob's well, and a woman of Samaria came to draw water.

The Jews and Samaritans had long ceased to have any dealings with each other; but our Saviour wished to put an end to this enmity, and to attract the people of Samaria to listen to His teaching. He therefore spoke to the woman, and told her all that she had ever done, and what she ought to do to worship God in spirit and in truth. She then left Him to return[5] into her city, fully convinced[6] that she had spoken with the Messias.

And many of the Samaritans of that city believed on Him for the saying of the woman, who testified, " He told me all that I ever did."

And they went out to Jesus, and besought Him to tarry with

[1] Doctrine, teaching.
[2] Sent forth.
[3] *Ad*, to; *traho*, I draw.
[4] Tetrarch, governor of Peræa, one of the four provinces, (that is, Judea, Samaria, Galilee, and Peræa).—*Neander*.
[5] From *restauro*, to renew, derived from *instar*, worth, value.
[6] *Con*, together; *vinco*, I bind.

them ; and He abode in their city two days. And many more believed because of His own word, and they said unto the woman, " Now we believe, not because of thy saying : for we have heard Him ourselves, and know that this is indeed the Christ, the Saviour of the world."

CHAPTER XXVII.

AND Jesus went up to Jerusalem to the feast of tabernacles. Now, at Jerusalem, there was a pool of water called Bethsaida, and near it lay a crowd of sick, of blind, of lame, of withered, all waiting for the moving of the water; for an angel of the Lord went down at certain seasons and troubled the water, then whosoever first after the troubling of the water stepped in, was made whole.

And there was a certain man who had suffered an infirmity [1] eight-and-thirty years.

When Jesus saw him lying, and knew how long he had suffered, He said unto him, " Wilt thou be made whole ? "

And the man answered, " Sir, I have no one to put me into the water when it is troubled, for while I am coming, another steppeth down before me."

And Jesus said, " Rise, take up thy bed, and walk." And immediately the man was made whole.

The man departed, and told the Jews that it was Jesus who had made him whole; and the Jews persecuted [2] Jesus, and sought to slay Him, because He had done these things on the Sabbath-day.

When Jesus was entering into Capharnaum,[3] a certain centurion,[4] who was a Gentile, came unto Him, beseeching Him, and saying, " Lord, my servant lieth at home sick of the palsy, grievously tormented."[5] And Jesus said, " I will come and heal him." The centurion answered and said unto Him, " Lord, I am not worthy that thou shouldst enter under my roof; but only say the word, and my servant shall be healed." And

---

[1] *In*, not ; *firmus*, strong.
[2] *Per*, through, thoroughly; *sequor*, to follow up.
[3] Capharnaum, a town on Lake Gennesareth.
[4] Roman captains commanding 100 men.
[5] Tormented, tortured. Literally, torn, twisted.

Jesus hearing this marvelled, and said to them that followed Him, " I say unto you, I have not found so great faith in Israel." And Jesus said to the centurion, " Go, and as thou hast believed, so be it done to thee." And the servant was healed at the same hour.

Now one of the Pharisees,[1] named Simon, desired Jesus that He would eat with him.

And a woman in the city, called Mary Magdalene, when she heard that Jesus sat at meat in the Pharisee's house, brought an alabaster [2] box of ointment, and she stood at His feet, behind Him, weeping, and began to wash His feet with tears, and wipe them with the hair of her head, and kissed His feet, and anointed them with the ointment.

Now the Pharisee was astonished, and said within himself, " This man, if he were a prophet, would know that the woman who toucheth him is a sinner."

Our Lord knew his thought, and said unto him, " Many sins are forgiven her, because she has loved much." And to the woman He said, " Thy faith hath made thee whole ; go in peace."

After John the Baptist had been beheaded in prison by the order of Herod, because John had reproved him for the many evil things which he had done, Jesus and the apostles went apart into a desert place to rest a while. And Jesus was followed by a multitude of people, anxious to hear Him and to see His miracles. And Jesus was moved with compassion toward them, because they were as sheep having no shepherd, and He began to teach them many things.

And when the day was far spent, the disciples said unto Jesus, " This is a desert place, and the hour is now past ; send the people away to buy themselves bread, for they have nothing to eat."

And Jesus saith unto them, " How many loaves have ye ? " And they said, " Five, and two fishes."

And He commanded the disciples to make them all sit down by companies upon the green grass. And when He had taken the five loaves and the two fishes, looking up to heaven, He

[1] Pharisees (Prushim) meant the separate or elect.
[2] A white, smooth stone, like marble. From Alabastron, in Egypt, where there was a manufactory of perfume pots. A softer substance, gypsum, or sulphate of lime, is now commonly called alabaster.

blessed and broke the loaves, and He divided the two fishes among them all, and He gave to His disciples to set before them, and they all did eat and were filled ; and they took up the leavings, twelve full baskets of fragments.[1]   And they that did eat were five thousand men.

Not long after this miracle our Lord fed four thousand people, and satisfied them with seven loaves.

CHAPTER XXVIII.

THEN Jesus departed into the coasts of Tyre and Sidon.[2] And a woman of Canaan came and cried unto Him, saying : " Have mercy on me, O Lord, thou Son of David, my daughter is grievously vexed with a devil." And He answered her not a word ; but she ceased not to pray and to beseech. Then Jesus answered and said unto her, " O woman, great is thy faith ; be it unto thee even as thou wilt." And her daughter was made whole from that very hour.

And Jesus and His disciples went into the town of Cesarea Philippi ;[3] and, to try their faith, He asked them by the way : " Whom do men say that I am ? "

And they answered, " John the Baptist, and some say Elias, or one of the prophets."

Then Jesus said : " But whom say ye that I am ? " Then the chief disciple, Simon Peter, answered and said : " Thou art the Christ, the Son of the living God."

And Jesus blessed Peter, and said : " Thou art Peter, and upon this rock I will build my Church ; and the gates of hell shall not prevail against it."

And after six days Jesus, with Peter, and James,[4] and John his brother, went up to Mount Thabor,[5] and was transfigured [6]

[1] From *frango*, I break. Signifies, broken bits.

[2] Tyre and Sidon, ancient trading cities of the Phœnicians, who dwelt north of Palestine, on the shore of the Mediterranean Sea. They traded as far as Britain, and sailed round Africa. Tyre (Tsor) means rock.

[3] Cesarea Philippi, a city in the district called Trachonitis, to the north of Palestine. It was called Dan by the Hebrews, and Cesarea Philippi by Philip, Herod's son.

[4] Greek for Jacob.

[5] Neat Lake Genesareth.

[6] *Trans*, across ; *figuro*, I colour, paint. Means, changed into a bright, glorious appearance.

before them; and His face did shine as the sun, and His garments became white as the snow. And, behold, two men were talking with Him, and they were Moses and Elias. And there came a cloud and overshadowed them; and a voice came out of the cloud, saying: "This is my beloved Son, hear him."

And one day as Jesus passed out of the temple, He saw a man who was blind from his birth; and Christ spat on the ground, and made clay with it, and anointed the eyes of the blind man with the clay, and said unto him, "Go, wash in the pool of Siloe." And the man went and washed as Christ bid him, and he received his sight.

And the Pharisees, who hated Jesus, because He rebuked them openly for their pride and their hypocrisy,[1] would not believe in the miracle, and they blamed Jesus because He did it on the Sabbath-day.

Now Lazarus, the brother of Martha and of Mary Magdalene, lived with his sisters at Bethania.[2] Jesus often visited[3] them when He came to Jerusalem; and He loved Martha, and her sister, and Lazarus.

When Jesus was in Galilee, Lazarus died, and was buried; and when Jesus came, He found that he had lain in the grave four days already.

And Martha said: "Lord, if thou hadst been here, my brother had not died."

And Jesus said: "Where have ye laid him?" And when He was at the grave, He ordered the stone to be taken away where the dead was laid, and cried with a loud voice: "Lazarus, come forth." And the dead arose, and came forth. And many of the Jews who had seen the things which Jesus did believed in Him.

The chief priests and the Pharisees gathered a council,[4] and said: "This man doth many miracles; if we let him alone, all men will believe in him; and the Romans will come and take away both our place and nation." Then from that day forth

---

[1] *Hupo*, under, or secretly; *krino*, I judge. Signifies falseness, doublefacedness, deception, sham.

[2] Bethany, near Jerusalem, on the north-east, means The Ford.—*Neander*.

[3] *Video*, I see; *visus*, seen. To visit, to go and see.

[4] *Concilium*, advice.

they took counsel together to put Him to death. And they sought for Jesus, and gave orders that if any man knew where He was he should tell, that they might take Him.

CHAPTER XXIX.

THE feast of the Passover drew nigh, and many people that were come to the feast, when they heard that Jesus was coming to Jerusalem, took branches of palm-trees [1] and went forth to meet Him, and cried, "Hosanna to the Son of David; Blessed is He that cometh in the name of the Lord. Hosanna in the highest." Thus was the prophecy of Zacharias fulfilled.

And the Pharisees said amongst themselves, "Behold, the world has gone after him." And they sought how to lay hands on Him.

And Jesus knew that His hour was come, and that Judas Iscariot, one of His twelve disciples, should betray Him.

Four days after our Lord's entry into Jerusalem, He celebrated [2] the Mosaic pasch with His disciples; and while they were at table, Jesus took bread, and blessing, broke and gave to His disciples, and said : "Take ye, this is my body;" and having taken the chalice, [3] giving thanks, He gave it to them, and they all drank of it.

And He said to them : "This is my blood of the new testament which shall be shed for many. Do this for a commemoration of me."

Our Lord then told His disciples that one amongst them was to betray Him; and He spoke to them of their mission, and of His love for them.

But going out, He went, according to custom, to the Mount of Olives to pray, and His disciples also followed Him. And He said : "My soul is sorrowful, even unto death."

Then taking with Him Peter and the two sons of Zebedee,

---

[1] A tree of the fern tribe, growing to a great height in hot countries. Some kinds of palms yield the fruit called dates. All Judea and Idumea were celebrated for their palm-trees.—*Butler's Ancient Geography*, p. 264.

[2] To pay honour to.

[3] *Calix*. Latin for cup or glass.

He retired to the mountain to pray; and, falling on His face, He said: "My Father, if it be possible, let this chalice pass from me; nevertheless, not as I will, but as thou willest."

And being in an agony, He prayed the longer; and there appeared to Him an angel from heaven, strengthening Him.

When He rose up from prayer, behold, Judas and a great multitude, with swords and clubs, sent from the chief priests to take Jesus; and he that betrayed Him gave them a sign, saying, "Whomsoever I shall kiss, that is he." Then they laid hands on Jesus, and bound Him.

Jesus was led before Caiphas, the high priest, and false witnesses were brought against Him; but Jesus held His peace. Then Caiphas said: "I adjure[1] thee by the living God, that thou tell us if thou be Christ, the Son of God."

Jesus said to him: "Thou hast said it." (St Matt. xxvi.) Then the high priest said: "He hath blasphemed." And they judged Him guilty of death.

The next day He was taken before Pontius Pilate, the Roman governor[2] of Judea, to whom they accused Him of stirring up the people; but Pilate sought to release Him, for he found no cause in Him for death. But the Jews cried out, "Crucify[3] him, crucify him." Therefore Pilate delivered Him to them to be crucified, saying: "I am innocent of the blood of this just man; look you to it." And the whole people answering, said: "His blood be upon us and upon our children." (Matt. xxvii.)

When Jesus had been scourged, the soldiers of the governor put a scarlet cloak about Him, and platting a crown of thorns they put it upon His head, and a reed in His right hand, and bowing the knee, they mocked Him, saying: "Hail, king of the Jews." And spitting upon Him, they took the reed and struck His head.

And after they had mocked Him, they led Him away to crucify Him; and bearing His own cross, He went forth to that place which is called Calvary, but in Hebrew, Golgotha.[4]

[1] *Ad*, to; *juro*, I swear. Means beseech.
[2] Called Procurator.
[3] *Crux*, cross; *fio*, I am made.
[4] Means the skull. It was the common place of execution at Jerusalem.— *Tholuck's Commentary on the Gospel of St John.*

There they crucified Him, and with Him two thieves, one on each side, and Jesus in the midst.

And Pilate wrote a title, and put it upon the cross, and this writing was: "Jesus of Nazareth, King of the Jews." And it was written in Hebrew, in Greek, and in Latin. (St John xix.)

And they that passed by blasphemed Him, and in like manner the chief priests and the scribes mocked Him, saying: "He saved others, himself he cannot save." And there was no one to compassionate the sufferings of our blessed Lord, but His mother, whose heart was pierced as by a sword, and His beloved disciple St John, and the two Maries.

And when the sixth hour was come, there was darkness over the whole earth until the ninth hour, and the veil of the temple was rent in the midst.

And Jesus, crying with a loud voice, said, "Father, into thy hands I commend[1] my spirit;" and saying this He gave up the ghost.

Thus by the death of the God-man as a sacrifice for the human race, the sin of Adam was expiated, and man became once more a child of God, and an inheritor of the kingdom of heaven. This is the mystery of the redemption.

CHAPTER XXX.

JESUS was thirty-three years old at the time of His crucifixion; and half the seventy weeks of Daniel's prophecy had elapsed. Henceforth the ancient sacrifices were abolished,[2] and the sacrifice of the cross became the only source of grace.

The enemies of Jesus now appeared triumphant; still they remembered that Jesus had said He should rise again on the third day. In order, therefore, to prevent any appearance of this miracle taking place, the chief priests and Pharisees induced Pilate to put a guard round the sepulchre,[3] so that the disciples should not be able to carry away the body of our Lord, and thus make it appear that He had risen.

But these precautions[4] were unavailing,[5] for the resurrection

---

[1] *Con*, together; *mando*, I intrust.
[2] *Aboleo*, I set aside, I do away.
[3] Tomb, from *sepelio*, I bury.
[4] *Præ* before: *caveo*. I take care. [5] *Un*, not: *valeo*, I am of value.

of Jesus Christ happened as He said it would, and confirmed[1]
all the miracles and the mysteries of Christ's mission on earth.
The Church celebrates this most glorious of all her festivals on
Easter Sunday.

For forty days after His passion Jesus shewed Himself to
His disciples, speaking of the kingdom of heaven, and eating
together with them.   On one occasion He appeared to as many
as five hundred of them.   When He had convinced them of
His bodily resurrection, and had given them His last instructions, He left them to ascend into heaven.

His ascension took place in the presence of His eleven
apostles, on the Mount of Olives.   Then His Divine humanity
ascended into heaven, and, as the Scripture tells us, " is seated
on the right hand of God," from whence, at the end of the
world : " He shall come again to judge both the living and
the dead."

Ten days after the ascension His apostles were all together
in one place, and suddenly there came a sound from heaven as
of a mighty wind, and it filled the whole house where they
were sitting.

And there appeared to them parted tongues as it were of
fire, and it sat upon every one of them.

And all were filled with the Holy Ghost, and they began
to speak with divers tongues, according as the Holy Ghost
gave them to speak.

Thus on the day of Pentecost,[2] exactly fifty days after the
resurrection,[3] the apostles began to preach and to promulgate [4]
the new law, as Moses received and published the old law fifty
days after the Exodus of the Israelites out of Egypt.

The blessed Virgin was with the apostles at the time of the
descent of the Holy Ghost ; and she continued on the earth
many years after the ascension, to edify [5] the faithful by her
relation of the miracles and the virtues of which she had been
witness at Bethlehem, at Nazareth, and wherever she had
followed Jesus Christ.   When the time was come for her to
receive her recompence in heaven, she left this world by a

happy death, and according to the tradition and belief of the Church, she was raised again, and her glorified[1] body carried by angels to heaven. The Church honours her Assumption[2] on the 15th of August. Her Coronation[3] is also honoured, and confers[4] on her the title of the Queen of angels and of men. She is all-powerful by her prayers to her Divine Son, and her protection is never implored[5] in vain.

CHAPTER XXXI.

THE Church had already spread abroad into divers countries, according to the prophecy of David, which said: "Their sound hath gone forth unto all the earth, and their words unto the ends of the world."

St Peter, to whom Jesus had said: "I will give to thee the keys of the kingdom of heaven," was then recognised as the prince of the apostles. After he had preached at Jerusalem, and established the Church at Antioch,[6] he fixed it at length at Rome, which thus became the mother of all the churches founded by the apostles. Hence the name of the Roman Church has been given to that society of the Faithful who, under the guidance of their legitimate[7] pastors, form one united body under Jesus Christ their head.

The Popes, as successors of St Peter, have inherited from him the primacy[8] of honour and of jurisdiction.[9] St Peter was imprisoned at Jerusalem by Herod, but an angel opened the doors of his prison, and set him free. He was, however, to die for the faith, and in the year A.D. 66 was martyred at Rome, under the emperor Nero.[10]

His brother, St Andrew, who had been like St Peter a fisherman, died as he did by the death of the cross. He was

[1] *Gloria*, glory; *fio*, I am made.
[2] *Ad*, to; *sumo*, I take. Taking up.
[3] *Corona*, a crown.
[4] *Con*, together; *fero*, I bear.
[5] *In*, into; *ploro*, I weep.
[6] Antioch, a large city in Asia Minor.
[7] *Lex, legis*, law. Means lawful.
[8] *Primus*, first. Means headship.

put to death at Patras, in Achaia,[1] where he intended to continue his mission after he had preached the gospel in Scythia.[2] He is usually represented on a cross, with its two extremities resting upon the ground. This apostle of Jesus was happy to die as his Master had done before him.

St James the Greater had been called to the apostleship at the same time as St Andrew and St Peter. He also had eagerly left his nets, for he, too, was a fisher, to become, according to the words of our Saviour, " a fisher of men." After the ascension he preached in Judea, and then, the tradition of the Church tells us, he went into Spain, and carried the gospel into that country. On his return to Jerusalem he was beheaded by the orders of Herod. His body was taken to Spain, and the capital of Galicia,[3] St Jago de Compostella, was named after him.

St John, his brother, was the youngest of the apostles, and the beloved disciple of Christ, to whom the care of the blessed Virgin was confided [4] by Jesus on the cross. He wished for martyrdom,[5] but twice was miraculously saved from it. A poisoned cup was rendered innocuous [6] by the sign of the cross, and he was therefore unharmed by it. Again, the Emperor Domitian [7] ordered him to be cast into a cauldron of boiling oil, out of which he came, not only uninjured, but even more vigorous than before. Inspired by God, he wrote the Gospel called after him, the Apocalypse,[8] and the three Epistles of St John. It is said that he rises like an eagle above all other sacred writers, recalling the visions of Ezechiel by the sublimity of his doctrine.

St Philip of Bethsaida devoted himself to Jesus Christ, and merited by his fidelity the confidence of his Master. He

---

[1] A country on the north side of the peninsula, called Peloponnesus, or Morea, in Greece.

[2] That part of Asia now known by the name of Independent and Chinese Tartary, with the neighbouring countries, Mongolia, &c.

[3] The north-westerly province of Spain, on the Atlantic, separated from Portugal by the Minho.

[4] Con, together ; fido, trust.

[5] Martyr. From marturion, a witness.

[6] Harmless. In, not ; noceo, I hurt.

[7] Ruled from A.D. 81 to A.D. 96. Born A.D. 51. He was the second son of

preached the gospel in Phrygia,[1] and several of his disciples founded the churches of Lyons and Vienne, in Gaul.[2]

Here St Bartholomew separated himself from St Philip, and went forth to evangelise the distant countries of Armenia and India. Tradition says that he suffered the cruel martyrdom of being flayed alive; he is therefore represented[3] by painters and sculptors with a knife in his hand.

St Thomas penetrated[4] even further into India, and his memory still lives at Meliapore,[5] and in all that country. He died pierced by an arrow. His zeal to do the work of his Lord and Master was a kind of reparation for the doubt which he manifested on the day of Christ's resurrection—a doubt, however, which has served to make it more certain to us.

Africa was evangelised by St Matthew, who was the first to write the history of the life and miracles of Jesus Christ. He went into Ethiopia, where already the treasurer of the Queen Candace had announced Christ. The greater part of the inhabitants of that country were converted, and have never since entirely lost the faith. St Matthew was beheaded.

St James the Less was the first Bishop of Jerusalem. His father was called Alpheus, as was also the father of Matthew. But St James the Greater was the son of Zebedee.

St James the Less was killed by the Jews at Jerusalem, by being precipitated from the walls of the temple. He has left us an epistle[6] addressed to all the faithful, and for that reason called Catholic, or universal.

His brother, St Jude, also named Thaddeus, wrote a short epistle, which, for the same reason, was called the Catholic Epistle of St Jude. He instructed Abgarus, king of Edessa, in the religion of Christ; he then preached in Mesopotamia, and afterwards going into Persia, received there the crown of martyrdom.

St Simeon, having travelled through Egypt, went into Persia, where he helped St Jude in his labours, and like him made

[1] A country of Asia Minor, now Turkey in Asia.
[2] France.
[3] *Re*, again; *praesum*, I am before, or present. Means shewn, or made present.
[4] Went on.
[5] Near Madras.
[6] Means letter in Greek.

many disciples. He ended his life, like the prophet Isaias, by being sawn asunder, thus confirming his teaching by his martyrdom.

The twelfth apostle, Judas Iscariot, betrayed his Master, and died miserably by hanging himself. He was replaced [1] in two ways.

After the ascension, when the apostles and principal disciples were assembled, awaiting the descent of the Holy Ghost, they nominated two of the oldest witnesses of the life of Jesus Christ. Of these two, Matthias was chosen, and St Peter numbered him with the eleven apostles. He afterwards evangelised [2] India and Ethiopia. [3]

CHAPTER XXXII.

ANOTHER apostle was called from amongst the most violent persecutors of Christianity by Jesus Christ himself; this was Saul, who had seen and applauded the death of the first martyr, St Stephen, but who became one of the most zealous preachers of that faith he had wished to destroy. As he was on his way to Damascus, [4] in order to carry out extreme measures against the Christians, suddenly from heaven there shone round about him a great light, and falling on the ground, he heard a voice saying, "Saul, Saul, why persecutest thou me?" To which Saul replied, "Who art thou, Lord?" And the voice said, " I am Jesus of Nazareth, whom thou persecutest." And Saul said, "What shall I do, Lord?" And the Lord said: "Arise and go to Damascus, and there it shall be told thee of all things that thou must do."

From that time Saul understood and began to teach the power of the grace of God; and as a reparation [5] for his past faults, he became the most indefatigable [6] of the apostles.

---

[1] Had another appointed in his stead.
[2] Announced the gospel to.
[3] A country of Northern Africa, south of Egypt, watered by one branch of the Nile, and now called Abyssinia. Its religion is a schismatic form of Christianity.
[4] Damascus is a large city of Syria, beautifully situated in the midst of well-watered groves and gardens.
[5] *Re*, again; *paro*, I prepare. To make up for.
[6] Untiring.

Having journeyed through Asia, he visited the island of Cyprus,[1] where he converted[2] the Proconsul[3] Sergius Paulus, from whom he took the name of Paul. He also went through the countries of Thrace,[4] of Greece, and of Italy. It is said that he even visited Spain. He wrote epistles containing the doctrines of Christianity to almost all the churches he had planted, and on returning to Rome, about B.C. 68, he was beheaded there on the same day that St Peter was crucified with his head downwards.

St Stephen[5] had been chosen by the apostles to help them in their works of charity as well as in their ministry. He was the first of the seven deacons[6] established for that purpose. But having one day spoken in the Sanhedrim of the divinity of Christ, and of the crime of His murderers, he was taken outside the walls of the town and stoned to death.

St Paul had an intercessor with God in the martyr St Stephen, and after his conversion he had the assistance of St Barnabas as a fellow-labourer, and was accompanied by him throughout Asia and the Island of Cyprus. On the return of St Barnabas to that island, at a later period, he suffered martyrdom.

There are two others amongst the disciples of our Lord who deserve special notice, as writers of the Gospels of St Mark and St Luke.

St Mark, disciple and interpreter of St Peter, wrote at Rome, from the mouth of the prince of the apostles, the Gospel called that of St Mark. He was afterwards sent to Alexandria[7] in Egypt, and was the first patriarch[8] of that city.

St Luke was a disciple of St Paul, and followed him in his travels. He was induced by that great apostle to write his Gospel, which contains the details of the life of Christ, and also the Acts of the Apostles, being a brief[9] account of the

---

1 Cyprus, a large island of the Mediterranean, now belonging to Turkey.
2 *Con*, together; *verto*, I turn.
3 *Pro*, instead of; *consul*, a consul. Proconsuls were Roman lieutenant-governors.
4 Now part of European Turkey, north-west of Constantinople.
5 Stephanos means a crown in Greek.
6 Deacon means servant in Greek—*diakonos*.
7 Built by Alexander the Great, King of Macedon.
8 *Pater*, father; *archo*, I rule. Patriarchs are Church dignitaries higher than archbishops, inferior to the Pope.   9 *Brevis*, short.

Church for the space of about thirty years. He preached and suffered martyrdom, like St Andrew, at Patras.

In order to appreciate the grandeur of Christ's mission, it is not sufficient merely to know the acts of our Lord and His apostles, we must study the doctrine which our Lord ordered them to preach. He commissioned them in these words : "Going therefore, teach all nations, baptizing them in the name of the Father, and of the Son, and of the Holy Ghost : teaching them to observe [1] all things whatsoever I have commanded you : and behold I am with you all days, even to the consummation [2] of the world." (St. Matt. xxiii. 18–20.)

The apostles therefore began to teach, and we have their doctrine embodied in the Apostles' Creed, which is therefore an epitome[3] of the Christian faith. There is a tradition which attributes this creed to the apostles themselves :—

"I believe in God the Father Almighty, Creator of heaven and earth ; and in Jesus Christ, His only Son, our Lord, who was conceived by the Holy Ghost, born of the Virgin Mary, suffered under Pontius Pilate, was crucified, dead and buried : He descended into hell ; the third day He rose again from the dead ; He ascended into heaven, and sitteth at the right hand of God the Father Almighty ; from whence he shall come to judge the living and the dead. I believe in the Holy Ghost, the Holy Catholic Church, the Communion of Saints, the Forgiveness of Sins, the Resurrection of the Body, and the Life Everlasting."

We have the development of the symbol, and all that belongs to the mystery of the Holy Trinity, in the Nicene Creed, which is said at Mass. The Incarnation and the Redemption are contained in the Athanasian Creed, which is recited [4] every Sunday at Prime.

CHAPTER XXXIII.

IT was not, however, enough to teach, the apostles were to baptize, and to administer [5] the sacraments instituted[6] by Jesus

-----

[1] *Ob*, against; *servo*, I preserve.
[2] *Con*, together; *sumo*, I take. Means end, finishing.
[3] A shortening; from *temno*, I cut off.
[4] *Re*, again; *cito*, I relate. I speak, read out.
[5] *Ad*, to; *ministro*, I serve.　　　　　[6] *In*, into; *statuo*, I appoint.

Christ ; for neither the knowledge of our religion, nor good-will, can sanctify [1] without grace, and the sacraments are the visible signs instituted by Christ to give us His grace.

Baptism sanctifies by purifying us from the stain of original sin, and thus making us children of God and of His Church. This sacrament is conferred by pouring water over the head and face of the baptized, and in saying : " I baptize thee in the name of the Father, and of the Son, and of the Holy Ghost."

Confirmation [2] is a sacrament by which those who have already been made children of God by their baptism, receive the Holy Ghost by the prayer and the imposition [3] of the hands of the bishops, [4] the successors of the apostles, in order to their being made perfect Christians by the grace which it confers on those who receive it worthily. The bishops also anoint the forehead in the form of a cross with chrism, [5] which represents the inward anointing of the soul in this sacrament with the Holy Ghost.

The Holy Eucharist [6] maintains in us the spiritual life of grace by communion, because, hidden under the species [7] of bread and wine, are verily and indeed contained the body and blood, the soul and divinity of our Lord Jesus Christ. Moreover, Jesus Christ is concealed under these two species, which represent His body and His blood apparently separate ; and in the sacrifice of the Mass, He renews the sacrifice of the cross, the merits of which are applied to us in the Holy Eucharist.

The sacrament of Penance [8] reinstates us in the spiritual life, when we have lost it by sin ; it was instituted in order to remit the sins we commit after baptism. Three things are required of us in this sacrament, Contrition, [9] Confession, and Satisfaction. Jesus Christ shews the power conferred by Him on His apostles to forgive sins, when, having breathed on them, He said to them : " Receive ye the Holy Ghost : whose sins ye

[1] Make holy—*sanctus* and *fio*.
[2] *Con*, together; *firmo*, I strengthen.
[3] *In*, on ; *pono*, I place.
[4] Bishop, from *episcopus*, overseer, inspector.
[5] Chrism means anointing oil.
[6] A Greek word meaning thanksgiving.
[7] Kinds.
[8] *Pœna* means punishment.
[9] *Con*, together; *tritus*, crushed.

shall forgive, they are forgiven them; and whose sins ye shall
retain [1] they are retained." (St John xx. 22–23.)

The sacrament of Extreme Unction relates to the life of the
body as well as to that of the soul. It was instituted by Christ
for the spiritual and physical [2] comfort of the sick, to whom it
restores the health of the body, if necessary for the salvation of
the soul. St James teaches the way in which this sacrament is
to be administered : "Is any sick among you? Let him bring
in the priests of the Church, and let them pray over him,
anointing him with oil in the name of the Lord : and the
prayer of faith shall save the sick man, and the Lord shall raise
him up ; and if he be in sins they shall be forgiven him." (St
James v. 14, 15.) St Mark tells us that the apostles anointed
the sick with oil, and healed them.

Besides the personal wants of the faithful, Jesus Christ has
provided for the general good of the Church.

The sacrament of Orders confers upon the ministers of the
Church the power to fulfil their functions,[3] and the grace to
exercise them holily. Consequently the Church is continually
governed and directed in the way of salvation, and the faithful are never without a visible authority, which they can on
all occasions consult, so as to escape all risk of error or
scandal.[4]

The sacrament of Matrimony was instituted in order to
bestow on those who enter into the married state a particular
grace, to enable them to live together in union and peace, with
mutual [5] respect, and above all to cause them to train up their
children in the fear and love of God, and thus to uphold and
propagate [6] the Faith by instructing their family, both by teaching and example.

In the third place, the apostles were to direct the faithful,
and were ordered by our Lord to teach them to observe or keep
the precepts which He had given them.

These precepts are firstly, the Decalogue, or the commandments given under Moses, which Jesus Christ declared it to be

---

[1] *Re*, back ; *teneo*, I hold.
[2] Natural, from *phusis*, nature.
[3] Functions, from *fungor*, I perform, I carry on.
[4] A Greek word, means stumbling.
[5] Mutual means one for the other, from *muto*, I change.
[6] *Pro*, before ; *pango*, to establish, to confirm. Means to spread.

His wish to have carried out in a more perfect manner. For this reason He taught that : "The law and the prophets are contained in these two commandments :

"I. Thou shalt love the Lord with all thy heart, with all thy mind, with all thy soul, and with all thy strength.

"II. Thou shalt love thy neighbour as thyself."

From this proceed[1] the three fundamental[2] virtues of faith, hope, and charity, which all have reference[3] to God as their principal object. They are called the three theological virtues.

By faith the soul receives the Word of God, and as soon as she is convinced that she has heard His voice,—as when Jesus Christ, holding the chalice, exclaimed, "This is my blood,"— she believes without further examination. But she examines[4] the authority which affirms[5] that God thus spoke ; and if the authority is legitimate, as the Catholic Church, she does not hesitate to believe. She says : "My God, I firmly believe whatsoever Thou hast revealed, and what the Catholic Church proposes to be believed ; and I believe this, because God, who is the sovereign truth, can neither deceive nor be deceived."

Hope dwells upon the power, the wisdom, and the goodness of God, who governs all things, and without whose permission nothing can happen, and she reposes therefore upon Him in all she requires and in all she does. God is her anchor of salvation. She makes use of natural means, but she asks for grace. She practises virtue, but she expects recompence, not from her own merits, but only from the munificence[6] of God's mercy. She says : "My God, I hope, from Thy infinite goodness and mercy, through the merits of Jesus Christ my Saviour, to receive eternal life, as well as the graces necessary to attain it.'

Charity is active faith : she beholds the perfections of God, and unites all her affections in Him as the source of all good, and as the end of all her desires ; for she knows that the only

---

[1] *Pro*, before ; *cedo*, I go.

[2] Fundamental—at the root, or forming the basis.

[3] *Re*, back ; *fero*, I carry.

[4] *Examino. Ex*, out of ; *ago*, I act. *Exigo* means to look into, to ask, to inquire.

[5] *Ad*, to ; *firmo*, to strengthen. To say as certain.

[6] *Munus*, a gift ; *facio*, I make.

true happiness is union with God. Her constant [1] aim is to please God, to observe His commands, and to follow His inspirations; and as she believes that whatever is done for the least of Christ's little ones, is done unto Him, she assists the poor, she consoles the afflicted,[2] she reclaims [3] sinners, and seeks out little children, and makes herself all things to all men to gain them to Christ. Then she says, with joy and with sincerity : "My God, I love Thee with my whole heart, more than all creatures, even more than myself, because thou art supremely [4] good ; and I love my neighbour as myself for the love of Thee."

CHAPTER XXXIV.

BESIDES the theological virtues, we find, both in the teaching and in the conduct of the apostles, the cardinal virtues, which are the source and the foundation of all the moral virtues. There are four of these—

Temperance restrains [5] the gratification [6] of sense within the limits of our reason.

Justice is the constant wish to give unto each that which is their due.

Prudence discriminates [7] betwixt the right and the wrong in our choice of action.

Fortitude [8] determines the will of man to defy, when necessary, the fatigues and the dangers which oppose him in the path of duty.

Thus we learn to correct [9] our faults, and to subdue our vices—as pride, avarice, envy, greediness, anger, and idleness —which are called deadly sins.

Jesus Christ told His apostles to watch and pray, from which we learn that it is not enough to keep from vice and to esteem virtue, but we must also pray to obtain of God the grace

[1] *Con*, together; *stans*, standing.
[2] *Ad*, to ; *flecto*, I bend.
[3] *Re*, back; *clamo*, I call.
[4] *Super*, above. Means most highly.
[5] *Re*, back; *stringo*, I bind.
[6] *Gratus*, agreeable ; *fio*, I make.
[7] *Dis*, asunder; *cerno*, I separate.
[8] *Fors*, strong; fortitude, strength of mind.
[9] *Co*, together; *rego*, I govern. *Corrigo*, to lead straight.

which the sacraments confer upon us, and for the help which we receive when we raise our eyes and our hands towards God and prostrate ourselves before the Most High in prayer.

Prayer is an elevation [1] of the heart to God, as a duty we owe to Him, and a means of expressing [2] our wants.

The apostles asked of our Lord to be taught to pray, and He gave them the following form of prayer, which contains seven requests, by which we express our desire to honour God as well as our solicitations [3] for our own welfare, and this we call the Lord's Prayer. We find in it the three theological [4] and the four cardinal virtues :—

Faith—	1st request—	"Our Father, who art in heaven, hallowed be thy name.
Hope—	2d „	—"Thy kingdom come.
Charity—	3d „	—"Thy will be done on earth, as it is in heaven ;
Temperance—	4th „	—"Give us our daily bread.
Justice—	5th „	—"Forgive us our trespasses, as we forgive them who trespass against us.
Prudence—	6th „	—"Lead us not into temptation,
Fortitude—	7th „	—"But deliver us from evil."— So be it.

The Church usually unites with this prayer the angelic salutation to honour and invoke [5] the blessed Virgin, in saluting her with the angel—

" Hail, Mary, full of grace ! the Lord is with thee—blessed art thou among women, and blessed is the fruit of thy womb, Jesus. Holy Mary, Mother of God, pray for us sinners, now and at the hour of our death." Amen.

Again, the apostles not only taught men to observe the precepts of the Saviour, but they also established a public worship, to render the duties of Christians more easy of accomplishment, by laying down certain external acts, to insure the sanctifica-

[1] *E*, out of; *levis*, light. *Elevo*, I raise up.

[2] *Ex*, out of ; *premo*, I press.

[3] *Sollicitus*, moved. Solicitation, movement, anxiety, strong wish; also petition.

[4] *Theos*. God : *logos*. science.   [5] *In*. into or upon: *voco*. I call.

tion of each as well as the edification of all. Out of this have
come the precepts of the Church, which at first amounted like
the decalogue to ten, but are now reduced to six. They are as
follows :—

1. To hear mass on Sunday, and all holidays of obligation,
and to rest from servile works.

2. To fast and abstain on the days commanded.

3. To confess our sins at least once a year.

4. To receive the Holy Eucharist at Easter.

5. To contribute to the support of our pastors.

6. Not to solemnise marriage at the forbidden time, nor
clandestinely,[1] nor within the prohibited degrees of kindred.

These are not the only precepts of the Church that we are
required to observe. We must also obey the canons[2] of councils,
the decrees of the Pope, the charges of bishops, and in general,
all that our legitimate pastors direct.

CHAPTER XXXV.

THE wise man, in the Book of Ecclesiasticus, gives us this pre-
cept—" In all thy works remember thy last end, and thou shalt
never sin," (châp. vii. 40 ;) and the apostles have in their wisdom
presented to Christians all those truths which are essential to
be known about their final destiny : these are death, judgment,
heaven, and hell.

Death is *certain*, though the exact moment at which the
separation of the body from the soul shall take place is to
us *uncertain ;* but we know that whenever the moment does
arrive, the soul will be called upon to render an account of its
actions, and that these will be weighed in the balance of Divine
justice, whilst the body will return again into the dust from which
it was taken. Neither health, nor youth, nor knowledge, nor
power, nor supplication [3] will avert this destiny ; therefore we
must be always ready ; for, as Christ says, " At what hour you
think not, the Son of man will come."

Judgment then follows, (according to St Paul,) and God will
require of each to render an account of the graces which he
has received, the faults he has committed, the good he has

---

[1] Secretly.   [2] Rules.   [3] *Sub*, under; *plico*, I fold. Bending of the knees.

neglected, the scandals he has occasioned, the time he has lost, and the idle words he has used. If the soul is in a state of grace, it will receive everlasting happiness as its reward—if otherwise, it will be condemned to eternal misery in hell.

Paradise is the abode of the blessed spirits, who, having been purified in purgatory from the least spot of sin, live for ever.

Hell, which is the abode of devils, becomes also that of the lost souls who are condemned to an eternal separation from God. This separation is the death of the soul, which consists not in destruction, but in suffering, for as Jesus Christ has said: " Their worm dieth not, and their fire is not extinguished." (St Matt. viii. 43, 45, 47.)

Such has been the doctrine of the apostles. They thus accomplished the mission which had been left them to do, not limiting themselves to writing, but preaching and teaching with the authority with which Christ had invested them.

We possess not only the New Testament, in which are the four Gospels, the Acts of the Apostles, their Epistles, and the A-poc'-a-lypse[1] of St John ; but we have likewise the traditions which the apostles wished to have preserved, and the institutions which they founded.

We have, moreover, the Church, that Divine structure, of which the faithful are the materials, and Jesus Christ the corner or head-stone. Upon this foundation rests Peter, to whom our Lord said, " Upon this rock (or Peter) I will build my church, and the gates of hell shall not prevail against it." It is built upon a rock, so that neither the storms of persecutions nor of heresies[2] shall ever shake it.

Jerusalem, on the contrary, has seen her towers, her walls, and her temple destroyed. Daniel predicted the fall of Jerusalem five hundred years before it came to pass. And Jesus Christ referred to the abomination of desolation spoken of by the prophet, when he said to his disciples: " This generation shall not pass away, till all these things be done." (St Matt. xxiv. 15, 34.) And accordingly Jerusalem was taken A.D. 70, at which date several of the apostles were still living, and St John's life was prolonged until the end of the century, when he died at Ephesus, under Trajan, about the year A.D. 101.

POST-APOSTOLIC [1] AGE.—THE PERIOD OF THE PERSECUTIONS.

```
A.D.
106. Third Persecution.
166. Fourth Persecution.
202. Fifth Persecution.
235. Sixth Persecution.
249. Seventh Persecution.
257. Eighth Persecution.
275. Ninth Persecution.
303. Tenth Persecution.
313. Conversion of Constantine and Establishment of Christianity.
325. First General Council of Nice.
```

CHAPTER XXXVI.

THE Lord had said to His apostles: "Behold, I send you forth as lambs in the midst of wolves." The first preachers of the gospel were therefore not surprised at meeting with persecution, which they endured and overcame with the prudence of the serpent and the harmlessness of the dove.

These persecutions were raised against them wherever they went; but the Emperors of Rome were the chief adversaries [2] of God and of His Christ. History records [3] ten epochs in particular, during which these persecutions were revived with increased animosity. [4]

The first persecution took place under Nero, A.D. 64, in which, as we have seen, both St Peter and St Paul received the crown of martyrdom.

The second general persecution was begun by Do-mi'-ti-an. towards the end of the first century. It was during this persecution that St John was brought to Rome and plunged into a caldron of boiling oil without sustaining [5] any injury.

The third persecution was begun A.D. 106, under Trajan, about fourteen years later. Amongst the first martyrs was St Simeon, Bishop of Jerusalem, who had reached his 120th

---

[1] *Post*, after. Post-apostolic age means the age immediately succeeding the apostles.

[2] *Ad*, to, against; *verto*, I turn, I go.

[3] *Re*, back; *cors, cordis*, the heart.

[4] Hatred, from *animus*, spirit, impetuosity.

[5] *Sub*, under: *teneo*, I hold.

year. Soon after, the celebrated St Ignatius, Bishop of Antioch, was taken in irons to Rome, and exposed to wild beasts in the Roman amphitheatre.[1]

The persecutions were resumed towards the end of the reign of An-to-ni'-nus Pius; and the illustrious martyrdom of St Felicitas and her seven sons took place at Rome A.D. 150.

The fourth persecution was revived by the Emperor Mar'-cus Au-re'-li-us, A.D. 166, and was very violent. Amongst the most illustrious victims [2] were St Polycarp, Bishop of Smyrna, and a disciple of St John, and St Justin the philosopher [3] and martyr.

The fifth persecution was raised by Sep-ti'-mi-us Se-ve'-rus, A.D. 202. The cruel and unrelenting [4] character of this emperor caused this persecution to be of extraordinary severity. It numbers amongst its martyrs Le-on'-i-das, the father of Origen, with seven of his pupils, at Alexandria; St Per-pet'-u-a and St Fe-li'-ci-tas at Carthage;[5] St Iren-œ'-us, Bishop of Lyons,[6] a disciple of St Polycarp, and many others.

The sixth persecution, A.D. 235, was severe, but brief. The Christians were now very numerous, hence the fury of the Emperor Max'-i-min fell chiefly on their bishops and priests. Pope St Pont'-i-an and his successor, Pope St An-the'-ri-us, were both martyred.

The seventh persecution was begun, A.D. 249, by the Emperor Decius. Pope St Fabian, successor of Pope St Antherius, St Alexander, Bishop of Jerusalem, and St Bab'-y-las, Bishop of Antioch, with many more, suffered martyrdom.

The eighth persecution was ordered by the Emperor Va-le'-ri-an about A.D. 257. Pope St Stephen and his successor, Pope St Sixtus II., together with four deacons, amongst whom was St Laurence, were sufferers under the cruel edicts of this reign; also the great St Cyprian, Bishop of Carthage; and some refer to this persecution the martyrdom of St Denis,

[1] *Amphi*, around; *theatron*, a theatre, a place of spectacle, a show-place. Amphitheatres were oval theatres, where the wild-beast fights took place.
[2] Victim, from *vinco*, I bind. It means properly the bound offerings sacrificed by the ancients in religious worship.
[3] *Philo*, I love; *sophia*, wisdom.
[4] Unrelenting, unforgiving.
[5] A large and ancient city in Africa, opposite Sicily, near Tunis, founded by the Phœnicians. It was conquered by the Romans.
[6] On the Rhône, in France.

or Di-on-y'-si-us, who was the first Bishop of Paris and called the Apostle of Gaul.[1]

The ninth persecution was authorised [2] by the Emperor Aurelian, A.D. 274 or 275. St Co-lum'-ba suffered martyrdom at Sens, in Gaul, St Momas at Antioch, and Pope St Felix at Rome.

The tenth and last persecution took place under the Emperor Dio-cle'-ti-an, A.D. 303, and it was the last and crowning assault[3] made by the imperial power on the Church of God. St Agnes and St Sebastian at Rome, St Quen'-tin in Gaul, and St Alban, the first English martyr, all sealed their faith with their blood. The slaughter of the Thebean [4] legion and St Maurice, their chief, is referred to this persecution. The Church was now to triumph visibly, and to overthrow Paganism. The blood of the martyrs was the seed of the Church.

CHAPTER XXXVII.

CONSTANTINE the Great was the first Emperor of Rome who embraced Christianity. He began to reign A.D. 312. Whilst fighting against Max-en'-ti-us, the son of Maximin, who reigned with Diocletian, Constantine prayed to the God of the Christians for aid, and his prayer was heard. As he was marching at the head of his army, a cross of fire was seen in the cloudless sky at noonday, and on it these words: "Through this sign thou shalt conquer."[5] It was visible to the whole army. This gave him confidence in the Divine protection; and after defeating the tyrant Maxentius, he entered Rome as a conqueror. He did not at once profess Christianity, but he published an edict of toleration, recalled Christians who had been banished, rebuilt churches, and gave the Pope the palace of Lateran as a residence. Thus Paganism gave way before the gradual extension of the holy religion of Christ, and the cross, which had been for more than three hundred years an object of contempt and detestation,[6] became the proudest decoration [7] of the hitherto

---

[1] Gaul, the ancient name for France.   [2] Permitted.   [3] Attack.
[4] It received its name from being raised in Thebais, or Upper Egypt.
[5] Ἐν τούτῳ νίκα.   [6] Strong hatred.
[7] Decoration. ornament. *Decus.* honour. modesty.

pagan emperors of Rome. In this reign the first general council was assembled at Nice, in Asia Minor, A.D. 325.

St Hel'-ĕna, the mother of Constantine, was a convert, like her son. She built many churches, and was a model of charity and piety. When in her eightieth year, she made a pilgrimage [1] to the Holy Land. Her great wish was to discover the cross on which the Redeemer of the world had suffered for our sins. Her researches were rewarded, and her faith recompensed, A.D. 326. She sent a portion of the true cross to her son, and enclosed the remainder in a silver shrine, to be preserved in the Church of the Holy Sepulchre, which she built, as well as two other churches, one on the spot of our Lord's Ascension, the other at Bethlehem, on the site of the Nativity.

In the year 330, the newly-built city of Con-stan-ti-no'-ple [2] was solemnly dedicated and named by Constantine, who removed the seat of government from Rome to the new capital in the East. This led before the end of the century to the final division of the empire into East and West, and to its rapid [3] decline. [4]

Christ had foretold that His Church would be always persecuted, yet never vanquished. [5] No sooner did external persecution cease, than heresies arose within it.

Ju'-li-an the apostate, a nephew of Constantine, made vain attempts to undermine and destroy Christianity. He had been brought up in the Christian religion, but forsook his faith, and thought, by degrading it, to bring back Paganism [6] in its place. In order to falsify Christ's prophecy, that the ruin of Jerusalem was to be final, he undertook to rebuild the Temple; but each time that the work was begun, the labourers were either killed by an earthquake, which buried them under the materials collected for building, or were dispersed by an outburst of subterranean [7] fire. Julian was not permitted by God to reign long. He was killed in Persia, in his thirty-second year, A.D. 363. Almost his last words were: "Galilean, Thou hast conquered."

[1] *Peregrinus*, a wanderer. From *per*, through; *ager*, a field. Pilgrimages were pious journeys to visit shrines.

[2] Constantine's city; *polis* meaning city in Greek.

[3] Rapid, quick.   [4] Decline, falling off. *De*, down; *clino*, I lean.

[5] Conquered. From the French *vaincre*, and Latin *vinco*, I conquer, I bind.

[6] Paganism. All the religions of the Roman empire differing from Christianity were so-called from the peasantry, *pagani*, who were the last to cling to the old heathenism.

[7] *Sub*, under; *terra*, the earth.

CHAPTER XXXVIII.

JULIAN was not the only enemy of His Church, vanquished by the Galilean. Va'-lens, (who persecuted the Catholics in favour of the A'-ri-ans,) Sapor, the King of Persia, the terrible A'-la-ric, King of the Visigoths, Gen'-se-ric, King of the Vandals, and the i-con'-o-clast[1] Leo II., the I-sau'-ri-an, were all formidable[2] adversaries of the Church.

Yet, in spite of all opposition, the holy religion of Christ was established.

The Church had triumphed over persecution by the blood of her martyrs. She had now to defend herself against the far greater dangers of error[3] and of corruption.

St Justin, St Irenæus,[4] and St Cyprian, were the earliest apologists[5] or defenders of the Church, in writing. Their works are valuable, not only as a defence of religion, but also as a record of many points of faith and practice.[6]

In the following centuries, there were many learned Doctors[7] and Fathers of the Church, but it will suffice to name the most illustrious in the Greek and in the Latin divisions of the Catholic Church :—

The four Doctors of the Greek Church are—

1st, The great St Ath-an-a'-si-us,[8] Patriarch of Alexandria. He refuted[9] the impious Arius and shewed an invincible[10] courage until his death. He died A.D. 375.

2d, St Basil the Great, Bishop of Cesaræa,[11] in Cappadocia. His firmness curbed the pride of the Emperor Valens. He died A.D. 379, six years after St Athanasius, and a confessor of the faith like the latter.

3d, St Gregory[12] Naz-i-an'-zen, Patriarch of Constantinople,

---

[1] *Icon*, means an image; *klao, klaso*, I break. Iconoclasts, breakers of images.
[2] From *formido*, fear. Means dangerous.
[3] *Errare*, to wander.
[4] Peaceful. From *irene*, peace.
[5] *Apo*, from; *logos*, a word or speech.
[6] *Pratto*, I act; practice, action.
[7] *Doctus*, learned; *doceo*, I teach.
[8] *Athanasius* signifies the undying. *A*, without; *thanatos*, death.
[9] *Re*, back; *futum* and *fundo*. *Refuto* means literally to mix cold with hot.

the friend of Basil,[1] whom he nobly emulated in his defence of the faith at Nicæa. He died A.D. 389.

4th, St John Chry'-sos-tom [2] succeeded St Gregory in the See of Constantinople. His eloquence procured him the name of St John of the Golden Mouth, and his writings are amongst the most renowned of the Fathers' for beauty of thought and style. He died A.D. 407.

The Latin Church produced—

1st, St Ambrose, Archbishop of Milan,[3] the friend and re-buker of the Emperor Theo-do'-si-us. He was also the master of St Augustine.

2d, St Jerome, Priest and Doctor of the Church, one of the most ascetic and most learned of the Latin Fathers. He trans-lated the greater part of the Old Testament into Latin, and corrected the Latin version of the New Testament. The translation is that known as the Vulgate. He died in the year A.D. 420.

3d, St Augustine, Bishop of Hippo,[4] was a convert to the faith; his name is both popular and illustrious, on account of his zeal, his eloquence,[5] and the number of works that he wrote. He died A.D. 430.

4th, St Gregory the Great, "the servant of the servants of God." The humility and magnanimity,[6] as well as the learned writings of this holy Pope, have made him the admiration, not only of Rome but of Christendom. He died A.D. 604, the same year as St Augustine of Canterbury, whom St Gregory had sent with forty other missionaries to convert England. This St Augustine, the apostle of England, and St Augustine the learned Father of the Church are distinct persons.

These are a few of the great men whom science [7] and faith have given to the Church, that they might confute [8] the earliest attempts of heresy to mar the triumph which the Church had gained under Constantine. But it is important to

---

[1] Basil—from *basileus*, a king.
[2] *Chrysos*, gold; *stoma*, a mouth.
[3] Capital of Lombardy in Italy.
[4] In Numidia, now Algeria, in North Africa.
[5] *E*, out of; *loquor*, I speak.
[6] *Magna*, great; *anima*, soul.
[7] Knowledge. *Scio*, I know.
[8] *Con*, together; *futum* and *fundo*, to confound.

remark that she needs neither great men nor any one person in particular for her continuance and prosperity : her institutions are sufficient for her necessities, and she feels the truth of the Saviour's words : "Fear not, little flock, because it has pleased your Father to give you all things." This little flock of Jesus Christ has become, in a spiritual sense, the mistress of the world. We shall now follow her progress century after century and see how she has covered the different regions of the earth with her pastures[1] and her sheep-folds.

CHAPTER XXXIX.

THE chief institutions of the Church are—

1st, The papacy and the episcopal body, which were instituted by Christ.

2d, The religious orders and the missionaries.

3d, The councils and the synods.[2]

4th, The schools and seminaries.[3]

In all ages, these means of preservation and of propagation have produced the greatest results.

The Popes[4] of the first century were all martyrs, after the example of their head, St Peter. They recommended to the faithful the practice of the "*evangelical counsels*," and from that time, the "*virgin martyrs*" proved the energy of their faith. The solitaries[5] of Mount Carmel followed the example of St John when he announced the Saviour, and the The-ra-peu'-ti[6] were remarkable for the austerity of their lives.

The *Council of Jerusalem*, in the year A.D. 49 or 51, abolished[7] the *observances of the Mosaic law*. The customs and the rules, then established, have given rise to the *Canons*[8] *of the Apostles*, and the *Apostolical Constitutions*. From this period we derive the institution of *Sunday*, or the *Lord's Day*, the celebration of the festivals of *Christmas*, or the Nativity, of *Easter*, of the *Ascension*, and of *Whitsuntide;* also the use of *unctions*,[9] of *chanting*,[10] and of *lights* in the services of the Church. In vain

---

[1] From *pasco*, I feed.   [2] *Sun*, together; *odos*, away. Signifies meeting.
[3] *Semen*, seed. Means nurseries.
[4] *Pappos*, grandfather in Greek.   [5] *Solus*, alone.
[6] *Therapeuo*, I heal. *Therapeuti* = ascetics.
[7] *Ab*, from; *oleo, olesco*, I burn, destroy.
[8] Canons mean rules.   [9] *Unguo*. I oil.   [10] *Cano*. I sing.

was the divinity of Jesus Christ denied by E'-bi-on and Ce-rin'-thus; feeble and fruitless were the efforts of the Nicholaites to render obligatory[1] a community of goods, as well as every other attempt to change or corrupt the faith. The purity and the truth of Catholic doctrine effaced every stain.

During the second century, the Popes and the greater number of the bishops received martyrdom; but "the Word of God is not bound." (2 Tim. ii. 9.)

Whilst St Justin and Ath-en-a'-go-ras each addressed an apology or defence of religion to the Romans, St Pantanus left Alexandria and followed the traces of St Bartholomew and St Thomas in India, there to announce the good tidings of salvation.

The bishops were ever watchful to uphold the wise discipline of the apostles, and condemned, in their councils every error of doctrine as it arose; thus the Gnos'-tic,[2] the Mont'-a-nist, and the Quar'-to-de'-ci-man heresies were opposed, and though they were not eradicated,[3] at least the faithful were warned against being misled by false teachers.

The festival of Easter was fixed for the Sunday after the full moon which follows the spring equinox.[4]

During the course of this century, the sign of the cross, fasts, prayers for the dead, the viaticum[5] given to the sick, and anniversary festivals came into use.

In the third century, the sovereign Pontiffs[6] increased the number of bishops and of missionaries. The Church of Gaul became very flourishing; most writers suppose that a church was established at Paris about this epoch, by St Denis, and soon after the planting of Christianity in France, there were almost as many colleges as there were cathedrals,[7] chapters, and monasteries.[8]

St Paul the first hermit,[9] St Anthony the patriarch of Cen'-o-bites,[10] and St Hil-a'-rion, his disciple and the founder of religious orders in Palestine, as St Anthony in the The-

---

[1] *Ob*, against; *ligo*, I bind. Means binding.   [2] From *gnosis*, knowledge.
[3] *E*, out of; *radix*, the root.
[4] Equal night and day, about the 21st of March and 22d of September.
[5] *Via*, the way. Preparation for the way.
[6] *Pontifex*, High Priest, literally, bridge-maker, from part of his duties at Rome in Pagan times.
[7] *Cathedra*, a throne, a pulpit.
[8] *Monos*, alone.   [9] *Eremos*, the desert.
[10] *Koinos*, common; *bios*, life. Life in community.

ba'-id [1] of Egypt, spread abroad a desire for the monastic life. The first monastery for women was founded in Egypt by a sister of St Anthony, in the year A.D. 270.

The heretics and schismatics, No-va'-tus, No-va'-tian, and Paul of Sa-mo'-sa-ta, who denied the divinity of Christ, and Ma'-nes, who maintained that there are two creative principles, were denounced,[2] and condemned in Rome, Antioch, Mesopotamia, and wherever the bishops found these errors had been taught.

St Clement of Alexandria, St Hyp-o'-li-tus, St Gregory Thauma-tur'-gus,[3] St Cyprian, St Pam'-phy-lus, wrote in favour of the Church, as did also Origen, for although at one time he erred in doctrine, he came back to the truth at last, whilst Ter-tul'-li-an after having advocated the cause of sound doctrine, employed his talents in maintaining the errors of Montanus. The advocate, Min-u'-tius Fe'-lix, pleaded admirably, in his "Octavius," the cause of Christianity.

The fourth century put an end, as we have before seen, to general persecutions, and the era of Diocletian, which began A.D. 284, scarcely lasted longer than the republican [4] era introduced [5] into France 1600 years later.

Pope St Mel-chi'-ades witnessed the conversion of Constantine, and St Syl-ves'-ter, his successor, had the happiness to baptize the first Christian Emperor, and with him to call together the first œcumenical,[6] that is, general council, in which 318 bishops were assembled, A.D. 325.

The Council of Ni-cæ'-a or Nice was a model to all such future assemblies, in which, illumined [7] by the Holy Ghost, the Pope and bishops—to whom Jesus Christ had said, "Ecce ego vobiscum sum:" "Behold I am with you always"—examine, dispute, and decide such questions of dogma,[8] morals, and discipline as have been submitted to them.

The Pope presided [9] by his legates, the bishops deliberated, and the emperor, after having been present at one of these sessions,[10] and having shewn his Christian and right intentions,

---

[1] Upper Egypt, near the ruins of Thebes.
[2] *De*, down; *nuntio*, I announce.   [3] Wonder-worker.
[4] *Res*, affair; *publica*, publica. Commonwealth.
[5] *Intro*, into; *duco*, I lead.   [6] Universal.
[7] *Lumen*, light. Lighted up.
[8] Thoughts, opinions.
[9] *Præ*. before: *sedeo*. I sit.   [10] Sittings. *Sedeo*. I sit.

promised to uphold with his authority the decisions of the council.

The council condemned the doctrine of Arius, which denied that God the Son was equal to God the Father ; and drew up a symbol called the Nicene Creed, published several canons, and settled many points of discipline.

POST-NICENE PERIOD.

A.D.
381. Second General Council at Constantinople.
383. Vulgate Translation.
431. Third General Council at Ephesus.
431. Conversion of Ireland.
451. Fourth General Council at Chalcedon.
476. Subversion of the Roman Empire and end of Ancient History.
496. Conversion of Clovis, founder of the Frank or French monarchy.

CHAPTER XL.

THE heresy of the Do-na'-tists was proscribed [1] by particular councils assembled at Carthage, Rome, and Arles,[2] which were sanctioned by the Pope. The Macedonian heresy, which denied the divinity of the Holy Ghost, necessitated the convocation of another general council A.D. 381. It was held at Constantinople.

Lac-tan'-ti-us, Eu-se'-bi-us of Cesaræa, St Hil'-ary of Poitiers,[3] St Cyril of Jerusalem, St Ephrem, besides the other illustrious doctors of whom we have already spoken, propagated and defended by their writings, the religion of which St Anthony, St Pa-cho'-mi-us, and St Basil traced the rules for those who wished to lead a more perfect life.

In the fifth century, Pope St Leo merited his title of Great, by his fine writings, as well as by his great deeds. He is classed amongst the Doctors of the Church.

A pious bishop named St Mammertus, instituted, in his diocese [4] of Vi'-enne in Dau'-phiny, the processions [5] of the Rogation,[6] which have since been adopted by the Church.

[1] *Pro*, before , *scribo*, I write. Means to publish as infamous, to forbid.
[2] In Southern France, near the Rhône.
[3] In the west of France.
[4] Diocese means district, province. *Dia*, through; *oikeo*, to manage or keep the house.—*Passow's Dictionary*.   [5] *Pro*, before ; *cedo*, I go.
[6] The days immediately preceding Ascension Day, and kept as days of prayer, devotion, and, in some countries, abstinence.

The monastery of Lerins was founded A.D. 409, one year before the death of St Maro, whose name is retained up to the present time by the Ma'-ro-nites in the East. This monastery is supposed to have been the first established of the kind ; it preceded that founded towards the end of the century by St Benedict, after he had passed three years of perfect solitude[1] in a grotto at Subiaco, about forty miles from Rome.

In France, St Ger-ma'-nus, Bishop of Aux'-erre (born 469), and St Geneviève, were possessed of many miraculous gifts, and Ireland was converted to the faith by St Patrick, A.D. 431.

Clovis, principal founder of the French monarchy,[2] was instructed and baptized by St Ved'-ast, and St Rem-i'-gius, Bishop of Rheims ; he merited the title of Very Christian King.

Heresy still continued its attacks upon the Church. Pel-a'-gi-us denied the necessity of grace, whilst Nestorius endeavoured to establish the error of there being two distinct persons in Jesus Christ, and, consequently, denied that Mary was the Mother of God. Eu-ty'-ches mingled the two natures, and admitted but one. The Nestorian error was condemned by Pope St Zos'-i-mus, and later, by the General Council of Ephesus,[3] which likewise proclaimed the Divine Maternity[4] of the blessed Virgin. This council was held A.D. 431, under Pope St Celest'-ine, and was followed, in 451, by the Fourth General Council at Chal'-ce-don,[5] under Pope St Leo. This council condemned the error of Eutyches, and declared[6] that in Jesus Christ are united *two natures in one person;* that He is *equal to His Father by His Divine nature,* and *inferior*[7] *only in His humanity.*[8]

St Paul-i'-nus, Theo-do'-ret, St Peter Chry-sol'-o-gus, St Prosper, and St Salvian, are the most noted writers of this century.

---

[1] Loneliness.
[2] *Monos*, alone ; *archo*, I rule.
[3] In Asia Minor, near Smyrna.
[4] *Mater*, mother, motherhood.
[5] In Asia Minor, near Constantinople.
[6] *De*, from ; *clarus*, clear. To make clear, to point out.
[7] *Inferus*, below.
[8] Manhood. *Homo*, a man.

MEDIEVAL HISTORY.

PERIOD OF THE BENEDICTINE MISSIONS.

CHAPTER I.

THE sixth century was rendered illustrious by many famous bishops, as St Ces-a'-ri-us of Arles, St Ful-gen'-tius, St Malo, St Gregory of Tours,[1] St Mé'-dard, St Ger'-main or Germanus of Paris, St Kent'-i-gern or Mungo, Bishop of Glasgow, who have nearly all left very valuable writings.

Early in this century the body of the great St Augustine was taken into Sardinia, and conveyed a little later to Pavia ;[2] but only a few years ago, about 1844, it was taken to Hippo, in Algeria,[3] the place of which St Augustine had been bishop more than 1400 years before.

Monastic institutions now began to spread very rapidly. St Benedict established his celebrated monastery at Mon'-te Cas-si'-no, between Rome and Naples, A.D. 529. St Gregory the Great considered the rule which St Benedict made for his order quite

---

[1] On the Loire, in the west of France.
[2] In Lombardy, on the Po.
[3] Now a French colony in North Africa.

a masterpiece of divine wisdom, and it became almost the universal rule of all other religious institutions.

St Comgall, in Ireland, St Rad'-e-gund, at Poitiers, and St Colomban, each founded different religious communities.

In 542, the festival of the Purification of the Blessed Virgin was instituted.

Heresy renewed its attacks upon the Church under new forms, or with newly-invented errors.

The Iconoclasts, or breakers of sacred images, continued to proscribe all use and veneration of them in the churches as idolatrous. This error was upheld by the weak and vicious emperors in the East. One of them, named Constantine Co-pro'-ny-mus, sent for a holy abbot, called Stephen, who lived near Nic-o-me'-di-a, and caused him to be brought to Constantinople, in the hope of gaining him over to his party, for Stephen was held in great esteem by the people, on account of his great virtues and holiness. The emperor tried to persuade him by argument, and said, " Why can I not trample on a crucifix without offending Jesus Christ?" Stephen then held up a coin which bore the emperor's effigy,[1] and replied, " I may, then, stamp upon this coin without insulting [2] you." He then threw the coin on the ground, and placed his foot upon it; and, when the people round the emperor rushed forward to chastise [3] this insolence, Stephen said, "If it be a crime to profane the image of an earthly king, is it no crime at all to throw into the fire the image of the King of kings?" The emperor, having no answer to make, ordered the holy man to be put to death.

The Mon'-o-thel-ites, or asserters of one will, revived the heresy of Eutyches with slight modifications. They taught that in our Divine Lord there was but one will and one operation.[4] Now the Catholic Church recognises [5] in our Lord *two distinct though inseparable natures*. She *recognises also two distinct wills—the Divine will and the human will—which can never conflict* one with the other, yet can never be confounded. And other errors arose, but circulated less widely than the great heresies.

Two general councils, both held at Constantinople, were

---

[1] *Effigies*, image. *E*, out of; *fingo*, I make.
[2] *In*, against; *silio*, I slide. [3] Chastise—*Castigo*, I punish.
[4] Work, performance. [5] *Re*, again; *co*, together; *nosco*, I know.

convoked, one in A.D. 553, which examined and discussed the heterodox [1] writings of O'-ri-gen and Theo-do'-ret. The other, convoked in A.D. 680, finally condemned the Monothelites, and carefully drew up its Confession of Faith against their heresy, as being opposed to the teaching of the apostles, to the decrees of Councils, and to the Fathers of the Church. This Council of Constantinople is regarded as the Sixth General Council.

In the beginning of the seventh century there lived in Mecca, a city of Arabia, a man named Mo-hamm'-ed, who, when he was about forty years of age, declared himself inspired by God to reveal a new religion. He drew up certain dogmas, compounded [2] of Judaism and Christianity, and, as he could neither read nor write, he employed a secretary. His pretended revelations were afterwards collected into a book called the Koran, which was intended to supplant [3] the Bible, and if such a thing had been possible, the fanatic armies of the false prophet would have succeeded, but the will of man cannot cope with God's revealed word. The Mohammedans do not date their era, as we do, from the birth of Christ, but from the He-gi'-ra, or flight of Mohammed from Mecca to Medina, which happened in the year A.D. 622 of our era.

The Holy Cross, discovered by St Helena, had been carried away by the Persians during their invasion of Palestine, in the reign of He-rac'-li-us, A.D. 614; but it was recovered, and restored to its place in the Church of the Resurrection at Jerusalem A.D. 628, and the Emperor Heraclius bore the cross on his shoulders, in humble imitation of our divine Lord, along the Via Dolorosa, or Way of Sorrows, to the top of Calvary.

The Picts in Scotland were converted by St Columba, and St Wilibrord evangelised Holland.

Religious orders still continued to increase. St John Cli'-mac-us, Abbot of Mount Sinai, wrote the "Ladder of Perfection;" St Gall, St Cuthbert, St El-oi' or El-i'-gi-us, St Ri'-quier, St Chad, St Bennet Biscop at Wearmouth, either founded abbeys, or extended them. St Val'-e-ry, first a recluse,[4] then Abbot, founded the monastery which still retains his name. Two

---

[1] *Heteros*, another; *doxa*, way of thinking.
[2] *Con*, together; *pono*, I place.
[3] To take the place of. *Sub*, under; *planta*, the sole of the foot.

towns were also named after him. St Aid-an of Iona and
Lind'-is-farne, and St Is'-i-dore, Bishop of Seville, St Ou'-en
or Au-do-e'-nus of Rouen, St Bede in Durham, and St Il-de-
fon'-sus of To-le'-do, all flourished, and many of them wrote,
in this century.

CHAPTER II.

THE eighth century witnessed the conversion of Germany by
St Bon'-i-face, from Britain, called the Apostle of Germany,
who sealed the truths which he announced with his blood.

Carl'-o-man, brother to Pepin, the founder of the first race of
French kings, became a religious in St Benedict's monastery of
Monte Cassino, and died in the odour of sanctity.[1]   Wit'-i-kind,
Prince of the Saxons, and his people, embraced Christianity.

The Popes during this time were labouring for the edification
of the faithful.   The dedication of the Pan-the'-on at Rome, A.D.
607, consecrated by Pope Boniface III. to the blessed Virgin
and all the martyrs, was established a century later by Gregory
III., as the festival of All Saints.

St Bennet of An-i-an brought back monastic discipline to
its ancient standard of regularity, which the unsettled state of
the times had much impaired.[2]

About 747, the celebrated and learned Al'-cu-in, an English-
man, gave an impetus[3] to education.[4]   At his suggestion,[5]
schools were established throughout France, the University of
Paris took its rise, and a universal wish for education was developed.

St John of Damascus wrote in favour of holy images, and
against heresy.   Leo the I-sau'-ri-an, and the Emperor Constantine Co-pron'-y-mus, maintained by cruel persecutions, the
opinions of the iconoclasts; but the Emperor Constantine, the
fifth son of the Empress I-re'-ne, together with Pope Adrian, I.,
endeavoured to heal the wounds inflicted[6] on religion by con-
voking the Second General Council of Nice, at which three
hundred and seventy-seven bishops were assembled from all

parts of the world. After due deliberation, they gave their judgment in these words :—" We decree that sacred images shall not only be set up in our churches and engraven upon the vessels of the sanctuary and on all ecclesiastical [1] ornaments,[2] but in private houses and by the wayside ; for the sight of the images of our Lord Jesus Christ, His holy Mother, the Apostles and Saints, disposes our hearts to remember and to honour those whom they represent. We are bound to render to them honour and reverence, but not the worship due to God alone. We may burn tapers and incense before them, as is usual before the cross and the holy gospels, because the honour paid to the image is referred to its original, and this is the doctrine of the Fathers, and of the Catholic Church." [3] Thus this sanguinary heresy was silenced for a time, to revive again with all its odious characteristics amongst the so-called reformers of the sixteenth century.

Pope Leo III. closed this century by crowning, on Christmas-day, A.D. 800, Charl-ĕ-magne,[4] king of France, as Emperor of the West. The memory of Charlemagne is honoured by the Church almost as that of a saint, by the University of Paris as its founder, by the magistracy,[5] who admired his excellent code of laws, and by the army who extolled his warlike exploits.[6] Both the Church and science owe him gratitude for having directed the bishops and abbots [7] to establish in all their churches and monasteries, either public or private schools ; although, in fact, these had been begun as early as the fourth century. The learned Alcuin was tutor to Charlemagne.

The piety of the ninth century prepared sanctuaries for the relics [8] of several illustrious saints—those of St Cyprian were transferred to Com-pi-ègne, of St Hubert, first Bishop of Liege, to the abbey named after him, of St Reine or Re-gi'-na, to Flav'-i-gny, of St Hel'-ĕna, to Haute'-vil'-liers in Champagne, and St Martin was taken from Auxerre to Tours.

A great misfortune was now in store for the Church. Whilst Russia was christianised, Constantinople became schis-

---

[1] *Ecclesia*, church, assembly.   [2] *Orno*, I adorn, beautify, decorate.
[3] From the " Manual of Church History." 1857. Burns and Lambert.
[4] Charles. *Magnus*, the great.   [5] *Magister*, master.

matic. Her patriarchs had often raised pretensions contrary to unity, and Pho'-ti-us, wishing to break with Rome, separated himself entirely from the Church ; but, as a compensation,[1] the converted Bulgarians repelled the enemies of the faith.

In 869, the Fourth General Council held at Constantinople, and the eighth of all the councils, confuted and excommunicated Photius and his faction, and also drew up wise laws for the discipline of the Church.

The demon of heresy thus confronted in the most important dogmas, attacked those truths which had as yet been undisputed. Got'-es-calc, a Benedictine monk, taught that Jesus Christ died only for the elect, and John Sco-tus Eri'-gĕ-na, wrote against the real presence. These deplorable errors have since been maintained and propagated in spite of the opposition and condemnation which they met with as soon as they appeared.

Hinc'-mar, Archbishop of Rheims, A'-do, Archbishop of Vienne, An-as-ta'-si-us the Librarian, and others, have preserved many doctrinal traditions in their writings, as well as contemporary and past events. Several of these learned men were professors, and, towards the end of the century, Re'-my, monk of St Germains of Auxerre, opened a school of philosophy in Paris.

Rome herself had more than once been afflicted by schism, when the Antipopes [2] disputed the authority of the legitimate Popes. This occurred still oftener in the tenth century, though without shaking the Holy See, or preventing the spread of the faith. The conversion of the northern nations of Europe took place chiefly in this century. Wi'-mon, Archbishop of Bremen, preached to the Goths or Swedes ; and Gil'-les, Bishop of Tus'-cu-lum,[3] converted Mc-is-las, King of Poland. Bohemia was evangelised, the kings of Denmark and of Norway embraced Christianity; St Ad-al-bert preached in Prussia, and received martyrdom; and in the year 1000, St Stephen was crowned king of Hungary.

In Spain, the Mohammedan Saracens [4] committed frightful persecutions against the Christians, and invaded other countries of Europe, and although the general ignorance which prevailed

---

[1] Atonement. [2] *Anti*. against; the popes. Opposition popes.
[3] Gilon, or Gilles, first a monk of Cluny, afterwards bishop and cardinal. He was an eminent poet of the twelfth century.
[4] The name given to the Arabs of Egypt and Asia who followed the reli-

led to much disorder and crime, yet in the cloister was found a shelter for science and letters, as well as a refuge for the persecuted, and for penitent sinners.

The monasteries of Cluny, Font'-e-nelle, St Myl'-iere, and St Den'-is, renewed a stricter discipline, and afforded general edification.

Greater authenticity [1] was given to the canonisation [2] of saints, in order to avoid all risk of superstition; [3] and in 993, St Ul'-ric, Bishop of Augs-burg, was proclaimed only after the most rigorous [4] investigation [5] of his cause.

Me-ta-phras'-tes, [6] O'-do of Clu'-ny, Flo'-do-ard, Leon'-ti-us of By-zan'-tium, even Sui'-das, [7] the Pope Syl-ves'-ter II., and Burch'-ard of Worms, prevented the surrounding darkness from enveloping [8] the Church.

PERIOD OF THE CRUSADES.

A.D.
1054. Election of Popes reserved to Cardinals.
1055. Schism of the Greeks.
1073. Pope St Gregory the Seventh.
1096-1099. Council of Clermont for the First Crusade.
1125. Ninth General Council—First of Lateran.
1147-1149. Second Crusade.
1179. Eleventh General Council.
1189-1192. Third Crusade.
1202-1204. Fourth Crusade.
1205. Twelfth General Council—Fourth Lateran.
1218-1229. Fifth Crusade.
1245. Thirteenth General Council.
1248-1254. Sixth Crusade.
1270-1272. Seventh Crusade.

CHAPTER III.

IN the eleventh century, the afflictions of the Church increased, and a Pope of ten years old was placed at her head. But by the singular protection of Providence, faith seemed more intense, [9] and in the midst of wars and political [10] troubles, the papacy was the only power which was respected, [11] so much so

---

[1] Firmness, genuineness.
[2] Process of raising men of eminent holiness to the dignity of saints.
[3] *Super*, above; *sto*, I stand. Exaggeration.
[4] Strict, careful.   [5] *In*, into; *vestigo*, I trace.
[6] Simeon Metaphrastes, born at Constantinople in the tenth century.
[7] A Greek writer in the reign of Alexis Comnenus.
[8] *In*, into; *volvo*, I fold.   [9] *In*, into; *tendo*, I stretch deeper.
[10] State or worldly affairs.   [11] *Re*, back; *specto*, I look.

that when Hildebrand, under the name of Gregory VII., announced, in the year 1073, that he would overthrow *every power which should rise up in opposition to Divine truth*, he succeeded in righting the vessel of the Church.

Towards the end of this century, the Crusaders[1] had made themselves masters of the holy city ; and in 1099, Godfrey of Bou-il'-lon was chosen King of Jerusalem, and proclaimed, with due solemnity, in the Church of the Holy Sepulchre. When a crown of gold was presented to him, the pious hero put it aside, with these words : " God forbid that I should wear a crown of gold in a city where the King of kings was crowned with thorns !"

But the infidels[2] continued to harass the Christians ; and a hundred and seven years after this event, they retook the city, and remain masters of it to this day.

The Ca-mal'-do-lese friars,[3] the monks of Grand-mont and of Vall-om-bro'-sa,[4] the Car-thu'-si-an, the An-to-nine, the Cis-ter'-ci-an,[5] and the Font-ev'-rault, orders calmed the tempest and encouraged the weak.

Be-ren-ga'-ri-us, Archdeacon[6] of An-gers, asserted that the body and blood of our Divine Lord are not really present in the holy Eucharist, but only in figure—thus was the heresy of the Man-i-chees revived, and though Berengarius, before he died, with sincerity abandoned this error, which was repressed for the time ; yet the seed had been sown, and it "reappeared when Protestantism revived so many exploded[7] and condemned opinions."

Gui'-do, a monk of A-rez'-zo in Tuscany, invented the gamut, A.D. 1009.

Ful-bert of Chartres, (1016,) Adh'-e-mar of Saint Ci'-bar of An'-gou-lême, Ra'-oul of Cluny, St Peter Da'-mi-an, Lan'-franc, Archbishop of Canterbury, Theo'-phy-lact, and Saint An'-selm, also Archbishop of Canterbury, kept alive the flame of pure doctrine.

---

[1] From *crux* and *cruz, croix* and *kreuz*, the cross.   Wars of the cross.
[2] Unfaithful.   Means here the Mohammedans.
[3] From *campus*, the field, Maldoli, near Florence.
[4] Vallombrosa—the shady valley—near Florence, in Tuscany.
[5] From Citeaux, in Burgundy, in the east of France.
[6] *Archo*, I rule ; *diakonos*, a servant, attendant.
[7] *Ex*. out of : *plaudo*. I strike with a noise.

St Anselm died at the beginning of the twelfth century, and eight years later, the celebrated St Thomas à Becket was born in London, 1117. He filled, with much glory, the See of Canterbury, and conferred upon it a still greater lustre[1] by his martyrdom.

St Bernard, called the last of the fathers, was possessed of the highest virtues and gifts. Though only a simple monk, his reproofs were listened to both by kings and popes, whilst he himself never offended against either humility or charity. He preached the Crusades, and thus contributed to deliver Europe from the Saracens, and France from feudalism. The instructions which St Bernard addressed to Pope Eu-ge'-ni-us III., probably aided Innocent III. in carrying out the many good works which he undertook towards the end of the century. St Bernard died 1153.

From the Crusades arose the great military[2] orders—such as the Knights of St John or of Malta, the Knights Templars,[3] the Order of St Lazarus, the Knights of Al-cant'-a-ra, those of St Michael in Portugal, and the Teu-ton'-ic order of Knights of St Mary; whilst the regular canons of Prémontré,[4] of St Genevi-ève, and others, kept alive piety, and a desire for retirement and for learning.

The errors and the disorders of the Al-bi'-gen-ses[5] recalled those of the Manichees, and, as they would neither submit to, nor respect public order, the law was obliged to oppose them by force.

The Vau-dois, or Wal-den'-ses, desired a community of goods, besides holding errors of doctrine condemned by the Church. The state of confusion which for two centuries had been caused by such repeated aberrations,[6] compelled the popes and the bishops to convoke numerous councils, of which four general councils assembled at Rome, in the palace of the Lat'-er-an. The first, in 1123, settled the question of investiture and elec-

[1] Splendour, literally light, from *lux*.
[2] Military means soldierly, from *miles*, a soldier.
[3] So called from the Temple of Jerusalem. Baldwin II., King of Jerusalem, gave these knights for their residence part of his palace, near the site of the Temple of Solomon.—*Feller, Dictionnaire Historique.*
[4] So called from their mother-house at Prémontré in France.
[5] So called from Albi, a town in Languedoc, in the south of France.
[6] *Ab*, from; *erro*, I wander.

tions, the rights of popes and emperors, and also discussed[1] the subject of expeditions[2] for the deliverance of the Holy Land.

The second was convoked in 1139 to combat[3] the schism of the anti-pope Peter Leo, and to re-establish discipline.

The third was held in the year 1179, against the Albigenses, or Waldenses.

The fourth council assembled at the beginning of the following century, 1215. It condemned numerous errors, and gave a decision[4] relative[5] to the Crusades. It also drew up important rules of discipline—in particular, the canon for annual[6] confession, and for Easter communion.

But before we quit the councils of the Lateran, it will be well to see how liberal ideas, tolerance,[7] and free instruction, were understood by the Church in 1179. It was ordered by the Council that schools were to be established for the poor, that no competent[8] professor[9] was to be refused, and that education was to be given gratis.

The twelfth century was instructed by the writings of Zo-na'-ras,[10] of Or-de'-ri-cus Vi-ta'-lis,[11] of the Abbé Su'-ger, and, above all, of Peter Lom-bard, of Richard of St Vic-tor, of Peter of Blois,[12] and of Gra'-ti-an.[13] The latter collected the decrees of the popes and councils, which form the first part of the canonical law.

[1] *Dis*, a part; *quatio*, I shake.
[2] *Ex*, out of; *pes, pedis*, the foot. A going forth.
[3] *Combattre* (Fr.), to fight.
[4] *De*, from; *cædo*, to cut, to strike—literally, to cut off, and thus to end.
[5] *Re*, back; *fero* (*tuli, latum*), to carry, to refer to.
[6] *Annus*, a year.
[7] *Tolero*, I suffer.
[8] *Con*, together; *peto*, I seek.
[9] *Pro*, before; *fiteor*, I speak.
[10] John Zonaras, a Greek historian, and monk of the order of St Basil. Died in the middle of the twelfth century.
[11] Born in England, 1075. Died 1143.
[12] Or Blosius. Died 1200.
[13] A Benedictine. Born at Chiusi, in Tuscany. Drew up a famous collection of decrees of the Popes. He finished the work 1152.

PERIOD OF THE MENDICANT ORDERS, AND OF THE GREAT
SCHISM OF THE WEST.

```
A.D.
1274.  Fourteenth General Council.
1309.  Popes at Avignon.
1311.  Fifteenth General Council.
1376.  Return of the Popes to Rome.
1378.  Great Schism of the West.
1414.  Sixteenth General Council at Constance.
1439.  Seventeenth General Council at Florence.
1439.  Reunion of the Greeks.
1440.  Return to their Schism.
1440.  Art of Printing discovered at Mentz.
1449.  End of the Western Schism.
1453.  Constantinople taken by the Turks.
1492 to 1498.  Columbus, in the service of Castile, dis-
        covers the West Indies and America.
```

CHAPTER IV.

THE thirteenth century was enlightened by the example and
preaching of two illustrious mendicant[1] saints, who drew after
them a multitude of followers.   These heroes of evangelical
poverty—St Francis of As-si'-si,[2] and St Dom'-i-nic—were the
chief cause of that revival which distinguished their epoch, and
the orders they founded have never ceased to produce the fruits
of salvation.   They divided the universe in order to spread the
gospel, or to restore the faith.   Missions date from them, and
every good work found its apostle.

The Religious of the Order of Mercy, the Ser'-vites, the Sil-
ves'-tri-ans, and the Ce-les'-tines; the Knights of St George, and
those of St James ; also the Do-min'-i-cans, the Clares, the Order
of Mercy, the Trin-i-ta'-rians, the Ur'-ban-ists, and the Au-gus-
tin'-ians, all contended against false doctrine, and the careless
lives of those in the world.   St Bon-a-ven'-ture and St Thomas
Aqui'-nas were at the head of this holy league, and were consulted even by the councils.

St Louis, king of France, adorned this century with his great
virtues.   His name is inseparably connected with the Holy
Land, and the seventh and eighth Crusades are due to his piety.
He died near Tunis, 1270.   In his reign the corporation[3] of the

---

[1] Begging; because poverty was one of their chief vows.   These orders
got their bread from day to day by begging it.
[2] Assisi, a town in the States of the Church, between Rome and Florence.
[3] From *corpus*, a body.

Schools of Paris took the title of University. In 1252 St Louis founded the Sorbonne. In 1289 the College of Har-court was founded by a canon and a bishop of that name; and three years later, the Cardinal Le-moine also gave his name to a new college.

The errors against the real presence were renewed, and the Church protested against them by instituting the festival of the Blessed Sacrament, or Corpus Christi, at Liege in 1246, which became universal in 1264.

This century terminated with the jubilee of Boniface III., afterwards granted every twenty-five years.

In the course of one century four general councils had assembled within the palace of the Lateran; and in less than thirty years two other general councils were held at Lyons. The first assembled A.D. 1245, and was intended to put an end to the differences between the spiritual and temporal power; henceforth the two powers were more clearly defined and understood. This council revived the zeal for freeing the Holy Land from the infidel, and also drew up a formula[1] of canons of discipline.

The Latin emperors took Constantinople in the fourth Crusade, A.D. 1204, and reigned till A.D. 1261. This gave rise to the hope of a reunion of the separated Greeks with the Church.

The Second Council of Lyons, 1274, or the Fourteenth General Council, defined that the Holy Ghost proceeded from the Father and the Son; it also took measures to put an end to the Greek schism.

Besides St Bonaventure and St Thomas Aquinas, this century produced the following writers :—St Anthony of Pad'-u-a, Pope Gregory IX., St Ray'-mond of Pen'-na-fort, Roger Bacon, Vincent of Beau-vais, Albert the Great, and two celebrated women, Gertrude and Mech'-tilde.

In the fourteenth century the Greek schism still continued to afflict the Church in the East, whilst another trial awaited her in the West. It was, in part, occasioned by the determination of Pope Clement V., a native of Bordeaux, to make Avig'-non, in the south of France, his residence.[2] The violence of the Italian nobles having driven him to reside there instead of at Rome, his successors continued for the following seventy

---

[1] Rule or system.   [2] *Re*, back; *sedeo*, I sit.

years at Avignon, until 1377. This gave occasion to the election of two popes, and the division lasted fifty years.

During the pontificate of Clement V., the order of Knights Templars had been suppressed[1] by the Council of Vienne, in 1311, being accused of having lost all discipline. This council also exposed many heresies, and condemned their upholders.

About sixty years later, John Wickliff, a doctor of the University of Oxford, taught that bishops have no pre-eminence over simple priests, and that confession is useless; he also denied the real presence in the holy Eucharist, and taught other errors, the tendency of which was to upset all subordination to authority.

In 1453 Constantinople was captured by the Turks, who put an end to the empire of the East. Its fate was regarded as a judgment for the obstinate schism of the Greeks.

Happily the religious orders continued to make obedience popular. The Oli-vet'-ans, the Jesuats, the Hi'-e-ron'-y-mites, practised severe rules; the orders of the Knights of Jesus, of the Star, and of the Dove, upheld and defended the rule of the Church; whilst John Duns Sco-tus, Raymond Lullius of Majorca, William of Nan'-gis,[2] William Li-ra, William Ock-am, the Cardinal Caj'-e-tan, John Tauler, A-mau-ry Au-ger, and the Cardinal Peter d'Aill'-y, maintained[3] true principles[4] in their writings.

The Popes Clement V. and Benedict XII. added fresh constitutions to the canon law, and St Bridget, as well as St Catherine of Si-en'-na, instructed by revelation, opened the mysteries of spiritual life.

CHAPTER V.

THE great schism of the West still continued to harass the Church, and the Catholic world divided its allegiance between the Popes and the Antipopes. France, Spain, Scotland, and Sicily, recognised Clement as the rightful Pope; whilst England, Hungary, Bohemia, and a part of Germany, supported Urban as the legitimate Pontiff, which in fact he was. It may be observed that, although opinions differed as to the right of each

---

[1] *Sub*, under; *premo*, I press.   [2] A Benedictine writer. Died 1302.

claimant,[1] there was but one belief as to the authority of the Apostolic See, and the necessity of union with it.

The cardinals and prelates of both parties met in synod at Pisa, 1409, and, in the hope of putting an end to the schism, they assumed the authority to set aside the existing claimants, and to elect a third as Pope; but as this act was irregular, the confusion continued, until, at the Sixteenth General Council at Constance, Gregory XII., the successor of Urban, and therefore the lawful Pope, resigned,[2] and Martin V. was elected in his place, and universally acknowledged, 1414.

The two anti-popes, John and Benedict, were deposed by the council, though the latter and his pretended successor had a few partisans, until the year 1429; but, after that date, all opposition to the unity of the head of the Church ceased.

The reunion of the Greek schismatics was also discussed at the Council of Basle, but in 1439 a general council was convoked at Florence, and was composed of Greek and Latin clergy. The emperor and the Patriarch of Constantinople attended it, and the Pope Eugenius IV. opened the council in person at Fer-ra′-ra. All the differences were gone into, and the emperor, the patriarch, and all the Greek prelates[3] except one, adopted the Roman confession of faith, and recognised the universal primacy of the Pope. Thus this schism was healed for a time, but in the following year, notwithstanding the combined efforts of the emperor and of the wiser amongst the Greek clergy, all that had been effected was annulled,[4] and the short-lived union came to an end. Very few years after this event, Constantinople, as we have seen, was captured by the infidel, who rules in it to this day, and the great Christian church of Santa Sophia was converted into a Turkish mosque.[5]

The errors of Wickliff had been taken up in Germany by John Huss and Jerome of Prague, who added others of their own invention. The Council of Constance[6] had condemned them, but their followers persisted[7] in maintaining their opi-

---

[1] *Clamo,* I call.
[2] *Re,* back; *signo,* I sign.
[3] *Præ,* before; *lati,* carried.
[4] *Ad,* to; *nullum,* nothing. Reduced to nothing.
[5] A Mohammedan house of prayer.
[6] Near the lake of that name, in the Duchy of Baden, on the borders of Switzerland.
[7] *Per,* through; *sisto,* I stand.

nions by force of arms; whilst in the Netherlands, and even in Italy, the dogmas of the Church and its discipline were attacked by schismatic preachers.

But the Church was not dismayed : she produced new orders and learned doctors. The Min'-ims,[1] founded by Saint Francis of Paula, were of great use, the Knights of the Golden Fleece, of St Maurice and St Lazarus, of St Hubert and St Michael, rallied round the altar and the throne.

The faithful rejoiced to see the holy shroud taken to Turin; the angelus[2] was established in France; the devotion of the rosary was more widely and zealously diffused, and the feast of the conception of the blessed Virgin universally celebrated.

Faust and Gut'-tem-berg invented printing, and gunpowder came into use, to render war still more sanguinary,[3] but as a compensation, the compass[4] gave greater security[5] to navigation.[6] We owe its invention to an Italian, named Fla'-vi-o Gio'-ja, a native of Am'-al-fi, near Naples.

The Catholic writers, John Ger-son, Saint Vincent Fer'-ri-er, Cle-man'-gis,[7] Saint Ber'-nar-din, Saint Lau'-rence Just-in-ian, Tos-tat, Cardinal Bess-a-rion, St John Cap-is'-tran, Saint Anto-ninus, Thomas à Kempis, Denis the Carthusian, Pope Pius II., Sa-vo'-na-ro-la, Fi-ci'-nus, and Tri-the'-mi-us,[8] rendered reli-gion more popular and attractive,[9] both to the learned and to the people.

[1] *Minimus*, superlative of minor; means least.
[2] So called from the angelic salutation in Luke, ch. ii.
[3] Sanguinary, bloody.
[4] *Con*, together. Fr., *pas ;* Sp., *paso ;* It., *passo*, originally from the Latin *passus* and *pando*, to spread out.
[5] Safety.
[6] The art of sailing, from *navis*, a ship.
[7] Nicolas de Clemanges. Died 1430 or 1440.—*See Feller in loco.*
[8] John Tritheme of Trittenheim, near Trèves. Born 1462 ; died 1516. He was a Benedictine.
[9] *Ad*, to ; *traho*, I draw.

MODERN HISTORY.

PERIOD OF THE COUNCIL OF TRENT.

```
A.D.
1513. Leo the Tenth.
1517. The Lutheran Heresy.
1530. Confession of Augsburg.
1533. The Heresy of Calvin.
1534. Schism of England.
1545. Council of Trent.
```

CHAPTER I.

THE numerous councils of the fifteenth century had remedied, by their protestations[1] and directions, the relaxation[2] of discipline within the Church, to which a past age of ignorance and barbarism had given rise ; but a reformer of a very different kind now appeared in Germany, named Luther,[3] who, under the plea of reforming the Church, preached down those very principles and rules by which reform is rendered possible, such as monastic vows, confession, acts of penance, &c.

Luther was by birth a Saxon,[4] a monk of the Order of St Augustine, and professor in the University of Wittemberg; he possessed great natural talents, but his proud and perverse[5] disposition led him astray. He counselled the Elector of Saxony, and several others of the German Princes, to confiscate[6] the property of the Church in their dominions, and the hope of a

---

[1] *Pro*, for ; *testor*, I bear witness.

[2] *Re*, back ; *laxus*, loose. Syn.—looseness.

[3] Luther is the same name as Lothaire or Lotharius, a frequent appellation of German kings, nobles, and people in the Middle Ages.

[4] Sepp (*Leben Christi*, vol. 6,) says he was not a genuine German, but of Sclavonic descent.

[5] *Per*, thoroughly ; *verto*, I change.

[6] *Con*, together, *fiscus*, a money-basket, a treasury. To confiscate is to seize private property and hand it over to the state or sovereign.

share in the spoils induced many of the nobles to join his cause : thus, he soon found himself at the head of a powerful and unscrupulous[1] party, allured equally by the love of gain and the freedom from all lawful restraint, which is always irksome to the corrupt heart of man.

Me-lanc'-thon,[2] Zuing'-li-us, Bu-cer, and others, were amongst his followers, but they soon split off to form sects of their own. In France, Calvin[3] rejected[4] nearly all the Sacraments, taught that free will was destroyed by the fall, and denied the real presence in the holy Eucharist; in this error going even beyond Luther, who never could quite shake off his belief in it.

Heresy seemed now to reign triumphant in Europe ; persecutions began in the East, also in the West, and above all, in England, where the fury of Henry VIII. and of Elizabeth shed torrents of innocent blood.

The concordat[5] between Leo X. and Francis I., published in the Council of Lateran, 1513, was much disliked in France, because it placed the nomination of bishops in the hands of the monarch. Religious wars increased in violence, and political intrigues were as usual mixed up with them.

In 1545 a general council was convoked at Trent,[6] and was attended by all the Catholic prelates themselves, or by their representatives. The Church wished to remedy the evils which neither the pontifical bulls nor provincial councils had effected. Lu'-ther-an-ism, Cal'-vin-ism, and all the other variations[7] proceeding from them, after being examined and discussed with the authority of an œcumenical council, were unmasked and finally proscribed ; definite rules were also promulgated for a real reform, such as the Church alone possesses means or power to confer.

[1] From *scrupulus*, a small stone, which, getting into the shoe, causes a hesitating gait.

[2] His real name was Schwarzerde, Black Earth. Melancthon is the same word in Greek.

[3] His real name was Chauvin (the Bald), meaning the same in French as *Calvinus* in Latin.

[4] *Re*, back ; *jacio*, I throw.

[5] Literally agreement. *Con*, together ; *cor*, the heart. Concordats are treaties between particular states and the Pope, who represents the Church.

[6] A town on the Adige or Etsch, in the Italian Tyrol.

[7] Different opinions.

POST-TRIDENTINE PERIOD.

```
A D.
1563. Council of Trent closed.
1582. Reform of the Calendar by Pope Gregory XIII.
1595. Persecution of Japan.
1618. Thirty Years' War commenced.
1713. Bull Unigenitus against Jansenists.
1774. Suppression of the Jesuits.
1799. Death of Pius VI. in captivity.
1801. Concordat with Napoleon.
1809. Captivity of Pius VII.
1814. His return to Rome.
1814. The Jesuits restored.
1829. Catholic Emancipation Act.
1848. Pius IX. at Gaeta.
1850. Re-establishment of the Hierarchy in England.
1854. The Immaculate Conception decreed.
```

CHAPTER II.

THE Council of Trent only closed in 1563, and its decrees, which form one of the most glorious monuments of wisdom and of doctrine, were printed and distributed, in order to console and strengthen faith, and to confound heresy and corruption.

The demon of heresy had in vain attempted to destroy the edifice of the Church, the sectaries had tried to introduce their errors, whilst scandals had glided within it; but the hand of God upheld His Church, and His angel drove away the perverse out of the true fold of Christ's flock. The sixteenth century is thus one of the most interesting epochs in the history of the Church. Cardinal Xim'-enes inaugurated it by the publication of the Polyglott[1] Bible. The first seminary was founded at Rome, 1565, by Pius IV.; and Saint Ig-na'-ti-us of Loy'-o-la gave the support of the Society of Jesus to the theologians who interpreted the Bible, as well as to the authority which maintained its doctrine.

The Thea-tins, the So-mas-ques, the Bar-na-bites, the Feuillants, the Ora-to'-rians, the Trinitarians, and twenty other congregations,[2] without counting communities of women, were established to help and strengthen those already in existence.

Saint Theresa reformed the Car-mel-ite nuns, and even the

---

[1] Many-tongued, that is, in many languages.
[2] *Con*, together ; *grex*, a flock.

Carmelite monks. She wrote like one of the Fathers of the Church. She died Oct. 4, 1582, the same day on which the reform of the calendar happened; the day after becoming the 15th. Pope Gregory XIII. rendered this service to science and to civilisation, and the Gregorian calendar was received everywhere, except by the schismatic Greeks and by the English, who retained a wrong computation,[1] in opposition to the Pope.

The seventeenth century brought to light many dangerous errors, which, under the appearance of a more profound[2] respect for the *grace of God*, tended to destroy the liberty or free will of man, and, as a necessary consequence, to overthrow religion.

Baius, a doctor of Lou-vain, had begun to teach erroneous doctrine, but submitted to the sentence which condemned it. His pupil, Jan-se'-ni-us, a Dutchman, and Bishop of Ypres, set forth maxims[3] still more dangerous; and after his death five propositions, taken from a book he had written, called " Augustinus," were proscribed. Many men of great learning and talent, such as Ar-nauld, Ni-cole, Pascal, and others, were misled by the subtle[4] errors contained in Jansenism, but very few at the present day hold these false opinions.

The So-cin'-ians, the Qui'-e-tists, the Freethinkers, tried to introduce wrong principles and doctrines. But the popes and bishops exposed the danger of them.

Saint Charles Bor-ro-me'-o, Saint Francis of Sales, Saint Vincent of Paul, Bos'-su-et, Fé-né-lon, Bour'-da-loue, permitted no error to escape their notice, and opposed and gave a check to the spirit of innovation by their writings or their institutions.

The Priests of the Order of Lazarists, the Congregation of Foreign Missions, the Sisters of Charity, the Religious of the Visitation, the Trap-pists, the Order of St Basil of Poland, the Brothers of Beth'-le-hem in Mexico, ministered to the religious necessities, both moral and intellectual, of the people, and in proportion to the spread of education, books were multiplied to supply the call for them.

Besides the great writers already named, we may mention Mas'-sil-lon, Male-branche, Thomas-sin, De Tille-mont, Fléchier,

---

[1] *Con*, together; *puto*, I make clear, I think.

[2] *Pro*, before; *fundum*, the bottom. Syn.—deep.

[3] Chief opinions, principles; from *maximus*, most, chief.

[4] *Sub*, under; *tela*, a web, a woof. *Subtilis*, fine; hence close, fine judgment and thought.

Rod-ri-guez, Su-a-rez, with a hundred others, who formed an imposing cohort[1] against ignorance and error. To these, if we add the productions of the Bol-land-ists,[2] of the Benedictines of St Maur, the translations of the Fathers and other ecclesiastical writers, besides the researches and discoveries relative to general and foreign[3] literature,[4] we see that the age of Louis XIV. was, under all points of view, very important.

We find in the eighteenth century the effects of the errors which had been so spread abroad during the last 200 years, in the denial of all revealed religion which now took place. The Deist[5] admitted no authority but reason ; the Pan'-the-ist[6] found his God in the universe ; the Atheist[7] acknowledged no God whatever ; and the Sceptic[8] looked on all truths as uncertain. These aberrations were advocated by Tol-land and Collins in England, Hel-ve'-ti-us and Vol-taire in France, and by the Mystics and Freethinkers of Germany ; whilst other fallacies were advanced by Swedenborg in his revelations. Spin-o'-sa deified[9] the world, and the mad revolutionaries of 1793 deified a woman, and called her the Goddess of Reason.

Whilst it was permitted by God that many hundred Catholic missionaries in China and Japan should fall victims to the barbarity and superstition of the people, it was also allowed that *irreligious civilisation* in Europe should raise scaffolds on which to sacrifice those who were still faithful to the voice of conscience, in order that the martyrs and confessors of the faith should once more seal the Christian dogmas with their blood, as well as prove to the world the necessity of Christ's Church, with her supernatural elements and her teaching, as the only bulwark of order and true liberty.

---

[1] A Latin term given by the Romans to a body of foot soldiers, answering to our regiment.

[2] From Bollandus, a Jesuit of Antwerp, who began the work, "Acts of the Saints," A.D. 1629.

[3] Literally out-door, from *fores*, an opening. It means stranger.

[4] Letters, that is, books.

[5] From *Deus*, God.

[6] *Pan*, all ; *Theos*, God.

[7] *A*, without ; *Theos*, God.

[8] *Skeptomai*, I look around. *Skepsis*, looking into, inquiring.

[9] *Deified*, made into God, raised to a God.

CHAPTER III.

THE nineteenth century began under happier influences. Rome recovered her pontiffs, of whom her enemies had hoped to deprive her for ever. Churches were once more opened, fresh religious communities formed, and pious works of all kinds begun.

The present illustrious pontiff, Pius IX., was born May 13, 1792, at Sini-ga'-gli-a, in the States of the Church, and was elected Pope, June 16, 1846, by the almost unanimous vote of the conclave[1] of Cardinals. His accession was hailed with the greatest joy and enthusiasm by the Roman people, and by the whole of Italy, to whom his enlightened mind and noble heart were already well known.

Among the leading events of the present pontificate are the re-establishment of the hierarchy[2] in England and Holland, the concordats entered into with several Catholic as well as Protestant powers, the return to a more zealous reception of Roman tradition, with an increase of attachment towards the Holy See, and, above all, the glorious outburst of faith which defined the dogma of the Immaculate[3] Conception, and raised it into an article of belief.

As the Church is militant[4] on earth, she will never triumph absolutely in this world; but, as she is the work of God, she can never be vanquished. Whatever persecutions the Church may still have inflicted on her by her enemies, we may feel sure that she will be sustained by the same spirit of endurance which has ever distinguished her from all heresies and sects. This she derives from the faith she has in herself, and in the promises of our blessed Lord, who, in transmitting to her His cross and sufferings, also conferred on her the Spirit of the Holy Ghost, which renders her the only source in this life of a blessed immortality in the next.

Notwithstanding every drawback, Christianity has increased . from the time of the apostles to the present century, and now the gospel is preached throughout the whole globe.

In Europe Christianity is almost universal, and even in those

---

[1] *Con*, together; *clavis*, a key, Council of cardinals. Literally, a chamber.
[2] From *hiereus*, a priest; *archo*, I govern. It means Church government.
[3] *In*, not; *macula*, a' spot. Spotless.
[4] Warring, from *miles*, a soldier.

countries which are not Catholic our bishops and missionaries are tolerated.

In Asia there are archbishops' or bishops' sees, at Smyrna, the Leb'-anon, at Babylon, A'-gra, Calcutta, Bombay, Pon-di-cher-ry, Verapolly, Madras, the Birman Empire, at Tonquin, in Cochin-China, Co-re'-a,[1] Manchooria,[2] and Japan; whilst missionaries traverse Syria, Asia Minor, Persia, Hin'-dos-tan, Thibet, and Tartary in all directions.

In Africa bishops preside over the faithful at the two Guineas, the Cape of Good Hope, and at Tunis, Trip'-oli, and Egypt in the north; besides our missionaries in Abyssin'-ia, Sen'-a-ar, Madagascar, and other islands, and the French establishments at Senegal, where negro priests evangelise their own people.

Newfoundland, Hudson's Bay, Nova Scotia, Upper and Lower Canada, more than twenty towns of the United States, the Tex-as,[3] the British An-til-les, Hay'-ti, Jamaica, Gui-an'-a,[4] besides Mexico, and the south of America, solicit the help of the Society for the Propagation of the Faith[5] for their bishops and missionaries, in order to carry on the work of regeneration. Oregon[6] has seven dioceses, governed by an archbishop-primate.

In O-cean'-i-ca our missionaries have penetrated from Van Diemen's Land to New Caledonia, and our bishops continue the apostleship of St Francis Xavier in most of the island-groups of the Pacific Ocean.

[1] A peninsula of Asia, situated north of China, projecting into the Pacific, and belonging to the Chinese.

[2] That part of Tartary situated immediately north of China Proper. The Manchoo Tartars conquered China and established the present dynasty about two hundred years ago.

[3] A territory to the south of the Mississippi, once belonging to Mexico, and lately annexed to the United States.

[4] British, Dutch, and French Guiana are colonies of those nations on the east coast of South America, north of the Amazon river.

[5] This Society is assisting in the apostleship six large communities, whose labours are devoted to the sta ions confided to them. The missionaries of the *Rue du Bac* are in Thibet, Japan, and Malaysia; the *Lazarists* are in the Levant; the *Jesuits* at Jamaica, Demarara, at Madagascar, and in the Rocky Mountains; the *Marists* proceed to Oceanica, New Zealand, and New Caledonia; the *Picpucians* to the Sandwich Islands, Pomatoo, and the Marquesas; the *Oblates of Mary Immaculate* to the Red River, to Natal, Texas, and Ceylon.—*Annals of the Propagation of the Faith.*

[6] A territory in North America, to the west of the Rocky Mountains, belonging to the United States.

The greatness of God is thus made manifest in the moral world, and in the sanctification of man. We will now contemplate[1] His physical works and their wonderful secrets, which science, guided by revelation, has disclosed to us.

CHAPTER IV.

THE earth we inhabit forms part of a vast system, of which the sun is the centre and luminary, having all the planets revolving round it at different distances, and in different periods of time.

Two principal motions belong to our planet, one of rotation[2] upon its axis, called its diurnal[3] motion, producing the succession of day and night, and another of progression [4] in space, or revolution round the sun, called its annual motion, causing the changes of the season.

The time occupied in the diurnal rotation is about twenty-four hours, and the course of the earth's annual revolution round the sun is completed in 365 days and about 6 hours. This forms the solar year.

The planets are erratic,[5] opaque[6] bodies resembling our earth, and, having no light of their own, shine only by reflecting the light of the sun. The primary planets are Mercury, Venus, Earth, Mars, Jupiter, Saturn, Uranus,[7] and Neptune.[8]

The minor[9] primary planets are Vesta, Juno, Ceres, and Pallas, with about forty more recently discovered.

Secondary planets are those bodies which revolve round their respective primaries as their centre of motion, in the same manner as the primary planets circulate [10] round the sun. The number of satellites [11] at present known are—the moon, which attends on our earth, four belonging to Jupiter, seven to Saturn,

[1] Karcher derives this word from *con* and *templum*, a space; a holy spot. It means to look at, or think upon.—*Schulwörterbuch der Lateinischen Sprache in Etymologischer Ordnung.* 1826. Page 247.
[2] Turning round, from *rota*, a wheel.   [3] Daily, *dies*, a day.
[4] *Pro*, forward; *gradus*, a step. Advancing.
[5] Erratic, wandering, from *erro*, to wander.
[6] Opaque, dark, shady; what cannot be seen through.
[7] Uranus means heaven in Greek.
[8] Mercury, Mars, Jupiter, Saturn, and Neptune were the names of heathen

six to Uranus, and one to Neptune. Others are supposed to exist, but are not fully confirmed.

Astronomers [1] consider the centre of gravity to be within the body of the sun. Thus, all the planets would soon fly into collision [2] and form one huge mass by the power of attraction, or centripetal [3] force, by which a moving body is urged towards a centre, but for the counteracting power called the centrifugal [4] force, by which a body revolving about a centre, or about another body, endeavours to recede [5] from that centre.

There are two kinds of centrifugal force, namely, the projectile force, which carries us onwards in our annual revolution round the sun, and that which bodies acquire by revolving on their own axes. For example, the annual orbit of the earth round the sun is described by the combined action of the *centrip'-etal* and *projectile* [6] forces; and the diurnal rotation of the earth on its axis, like a wheel round the axle, gives to all its parts a *centrif'-ugal* force proportioned to its velocity. [7]

The earth is not a perfect sphere, but is somewhat flattened at the poles. The form of the earth is consequently an oblate [8] spheroid. [9]

In order to form some idea of the vast bulk of the planets, and of their orbits, it will suffice to know that the earth is about 24,856 miles in circumference, and that the volume of the sun is 1,401,910 times that of the earth; also that the distance of the sun from the earth is more than ninety-five millions of miles, whilst Uranus is twenty times more distant.

The earth's satellite, the moon, is by far the nearest of all the heavenly bodies, being only 238,650 miles from our globe. Though the motion of the earth in its orbit be not uniform, [10] yet it is regulated by a certain immutable law, from which it never deviates. [11] These facts cannot but remind us of the

---

[1] *Aster*, a star; *nomos*, the law. Men knowing the laws of stars.
[2] *Con*, together; *laedo*, I injure, hurt.
[3] *Kentron*, the middle point; *pipto*, I fall.
[4] *Kentron*, the middle; *fugo*, I fly.
[5] *Re*, back; *cedo*, I go.
[6] *Pro*, forward; *jacio*, I throw.
[7] *Velox*, quick.
[8] Flattened at the poles.
[9] A body like a sphere, but not exactly round.
[10] From *una*, one; *forma*, form. Means unchanging.
[11] *De*, out of; *via*, the way. Goes aside.

promise made to Noe after the Deluge, that "While the earth remaineth, seed-time and harvest, and cold and heat, and summer and winter, and day and night, shall not cease."

The different limits to which the light of the sun reaches, during the movement of the earth round the sun, are marked on our maps by the tropical and polar circles.

The extremities[1] of the axis of the earth are called poles, one of which is the North or Arctic[2] Pole, the other the South or Ant-arc-tic[3] Pole. The circle which is supposed to divide the earth into two equal parts, and at an equal distance from each pole, is called the equator.[4] The tropic,[5] which lies to the north of the equator, is named the tropic of Cancer;[6] the other, to the south, the tropic of Ca-pri-corn.[7]

CHAPTER V.

THE earth is enveloped by a fluid called the atmosphere, upon which respiring beings depend for vitality. The extent of this wonderful and benign envelope is not exactly known, but its density diminishes[8] as we ascend from the surface, so that on the tops of high mountains it becomes so rare as to interfere with the functions[9] of existence.

Though the atmosphere[10] is invisible[11] and impalpable,[12] yet it is subject to the law of attraction, which draws it towards the centre of the globe by the force of gravity.[13]

All solid bodies are, from the same cause, prevented from leaving the surface of the earth altogether, and people move round in all directions without any danger of falling from it; therefore two men placed exactly in corresponding parts of

[1] Ends. *Extremus*, superlative of *exterus*, outside.
[2] *Arctos*, a bear; hence North Pole, from the constellation of the Bear.
[3] *Anti*, opposed to, against the arctic.
[4] From *æquus*, even. A line dividing the earth into two equal parts.
[5] *Tropos*, turning.
[6] Cancer, the crab; a constellation and sign of the zodiac.
[7] Capricorn, a goat; another sign of the zodiac.
[8] *De*, from; *minus*, less. To make less.
[9] *Fungor*, I do, I perform. Function, performance.
[10] *Atmos*, mist, vapour. Atmosphere = air.
[11] Unseen. *In*, not; *visus*, seen.
[12] *In*, not; *palpo*, I touch.
[13] Weight, from *gravis*, heavy.

opposite hemispheres[1] will walk with their feet turned towards each other. This is the origin of the term an-tip -ŏ-dĕs.[2]

As the daily rotation of our globe on its axis produces the succession of day and night, we in consequence have the sun-light when turned towards him during the day, and the moon-light when we are turned from him during the night, the light given by the moon being the reflected light of the sun.

The moon is the most valuable of the planets in relation to mankind; it serves as a guide to the mariner[3] in the trackless path of the ocean, and its influence, combined with that of the sun, produces the tides.

The moon rotates on its axis, and also revolves in its orbit round the earth. This latter movement it performs in about twenty-seven days, returning nearly during that period to the point of departure. The synodical[4] or lunar month is longer by about two days and a half than the other, which is termed a sidereal revolution.

The sun has also a rotation about its axis, which it completes in about twenty-five days and a half.

The months of the year are called solar[5] months. The year is divided into twelve of these months, in order to approach as near as possible the lunar period used by the Jews and other people. Since the Gregorian[6] reform of the calendar, the solar year is certainly the most convenient measure of time.

The eclipse[7] of the moon is occasioned by an interposition[8] of the earth between the sun and the moon; consequently all eclipses of the moon happen at full moon.

An eclipse of the sun results from the passage of the moon between the earth and the sun, when the body of the moon is exactly interposed between us and the sun. All eclipses of the sun happen at the time of new moon. Nothing can be more simple or natural than these phenomena.[9] It is a mere

---

[1] *Hemi*, half; *sphere*, a ball,
[2] *Anti*, against; *pous*, a foot.
[3] Syn.—sailor. From *mare*, the Latin for sea.
[4] From *sun*, together; *odos*, the way.
[5] Literally sunny, from *sol*, the sun.
[6] See page 97.
[7] *Ex*, out of; *leipsis*, leaving. Leaving out, omission.
[8] *Inter*, between; *pono*, I place.
[9] Appearances. From *phaino*, I appear.

superstition to imagine, as people formerly did, that they are the forerunners of great calamities.[1]

These few remarks only touch upon a very small portion of that vast universe which the Divine power has formed. Beyond our own solar system, itself so vast, there exist in those distant regions of space, known as the sidereal[2] heavens, countless stars, reaching even to infinity. Even with the naked eye we can perceive how numerous are the brilliant[3] specks of light so lavishly scattered in all directions; but when the depths of the heavens are sounded by means of the telescope,[4] we perceive that those stars which are seen by the unassisted vision[5] form one cluster out of many thousands. Our sun is but one out of those myriads of objects shining by their own light, being the centre of great systems like ours, each performing in its sphere the same functions to the worlds revolving around its concentrated light and heat which the sun performs for us.

> "These are Thy glorious works, Parent of good !
> Almighty ! Thine this universal frame,
> Thus wondrous fair; Thyself how wondrous then !
> Unspeakable ! who sitt'st above these heavens,
> To us invisible, or dimly seen
> In these thy lowest works ; yet these declare
> Thy goodness beyond thought, and power divine."

CHAPTER VI.

NOT only does the creation of the world excite our admiration, but its preservation and the beneficent[6] providence of God, which provides for all our wants, ought to touch our hearts and inspire in us the deepest gratitude.

But the earth is not always to subsist. The time will come when this world shall perish. For, as St Peter writes, "The heavens shall pass away with great violence, and the elements shall be melted with heat, and the earth, and the works that are in it, shall be burned up."

[1] Misfortunes.
[2] Starry. From *sidus*, a star.
[3] Shining. From *briller* (Fr.), to shine.
[4] From *telos*, the end; *skopeo*, I see, I detect,
[5] Sight. From *video*, I see.
[6] *Bene*, well, good; *facio*, I do.

"And then the Son of man shall come in his majesty, and all the angels with him : then shall he sit upon the seat of his majesty.

"And all nations shall be gathered together before him, and he shall separate them one from another as the shepherd separateth the sheep from the goats ; and he shall set the sheep on his right hand, but the goats on his left. Then the king shall say to them that shall be on his right hand, 'Come, ye blessed of my Father, possess ye the kingdom prepared for you from the foundation of the world.' Then he shall say to them also that shall be on his left hand, 'Depart from me, you cursed, into everlasting fire, which was prepared for the devil and his angels.' And these shall go into everlasting punishment; but the just into life everlasting."

It is in these words that Scripture represents to us the general resurrection [1] at the end of the world, and the last judgment.

The Apostle St Paul explains, with regard to the resurrection of the elect who die in a state of grace, that they are the first to rise again. Then, speaking in general, he says, "We shall all indeed rise again, but we shall not all be changed." He thus gives us to understand that the bodies of the saints will be glorified, whilst those of the reprobate [2] will be in a state of shame and of suffering.

St John, in his Apocalypse, describes, in magnificent language, and under symbolical figures, the glory and the happiness of heaven, that place of spiritual delights where the elect enjoy the beatific vision, and which is called by the prophets and apostles paradise :—

"Behold there was a throne set in heaven, and upon the throne one sitting. And he that sat was to the sight like the jasper and the sardine stone, and there was a rainbow round about the throne, in sight like unto an emerald. And round about the throne were four and twenty seats; and upon the seats four and twenty ancients sitting, clothed in white garments, and on their heads were crowns of gold. And from the throne proceeded lightnings, and voices, and thunders; and there were seven lamps burning before the throne, which are

[1] *Re*, again; *surrigo*, I rise.
[2] *Re*, again, or back; *probo*, I prove.

the seven spirits of God. And voices were heard crying without ceasing, 'Holy, holy, holy Lord God Almighty, who was, and who is, and who is to come.' . . . And I heard the voice of many angels round about the throne, ... crying, with a loud voice, The Lamb that was slain is worthy to receive power, and divinity, and wisdom, and strength, and honour, and glory, and benediction.[1] And I heard all saying, To him that sitteth on the throne, and to the Lamb, benediction, and honour, and glory, and power, for ever and ever.

"And a great sign appeared in heaven: a woman clothed with the sun, and the moon under her feet, and on her head a crown of twelve stars. . . . . And there was a great battle in heaven, Michael and his angels fought with the dragon, and the dragon fought and his angels; and they prevailed not, neither was their place found any more in heaven. . . . . And lo, a lamb stood upon Mount Sion, and with him an hundred forty thousand, and having his name and the name of his Father on their foreheads. And I heard, as it were, the voice of a great multitude, crying, Alleluia. . . . . And I heard a great voice from the throne, saying, Behold the tabernacle of God with men, and he will dwell with them, and they shall be his people: and God himself with them shall be their God. And God shall wipe away all tears from their eyes, and death shall be no more, nor mourning, nor crying, nor sorrow shall be any more. . . . . And night shall be no more; and they shall not need the light of the lamp, nor the light of the sun, because the Lord God shall enlighten them, and they shall reign for ever and ever."

[1] *Bene*, well; *dico*, I say.

THE END.